THE GUNSMITH

433

Little Amsterdam

**Books by J.R. Roberts
(Robert J. Randisi)**

COMING SOON!

The Gunsmith
434 – The Butcher of the Bayou

The Gunsmith series

The Lady Gunsmith series

Angel Eyes series

Tracker series

Mountain Jack Pike series

For more information visit:
www.speakingvolumes.us

THE GUNSMITH

433

Little Amsterdam

J.R. Roberts

SPEAKING VOLUMES, LLC
NAPLES, FLORIDA
2018

Little Amsterdam

ISBN 978-1-62815-754-3

Chapter One

Of all the regions Clint had visited that lay west of the Mississippi River—states, or places that had become states since he was there—he had probably spent the least amount of time in Minnesota. Or Idaho. Or even Alaska. But Minnesota was certainly on that list.

He much preferred the Southwest region of the country. But since he had just finished some business in the Dakota Territory, specifically Sioux Falls, and was near the borders of Iowa and Minnesota, he decided to give Minnesota a chance to capture his attention. Besides, he had no place else to go at the moment, nothing to do, nobody waiting for him. In other words, time to kill.

Later, he'd remember what an unfortunate phrase that turned out to be.

***

The first thing of interest Clint saw in Minnesota was a sign that read LITTLE AMSTERDAM 5 miles. Clint knew from his visits to New York City that the island of Manhattan had once been ruled by the Dutch and called New Amsterdam. The only thing he really knew about Minnesota was that it had become a state in 1858. But he found this sign interesting and headed that way.

The second thing he found interesting about Minnesota was something he saw when he reached Little Amsterdam, but that would come later.

***

When Clint found Little Amsterdam, he was impressed. Although it looked as if it had sprung up recently, with many of the buildings still smelling of newly cut wood, it also had the appearance of a thriving community. The main street he rode down was busy and lined with stores—some of which he had never seen in Western towns before. There was a bakery, a tea shop, a shoe store, a candy store, and a soda fountain. Luckily, he also came across a saloon, so he wasn't going to have to quench his thirst with an ice cream soda.

The place had the rather obvious name of The Dutchman Saloon. He left Eclipse standing out front, not bothering to tie him off because he knew the Darley wouldn't go anywhere and went inside.

It was early in the day and the saloon wasn't busy. It was cavernous on the inside, with high ceilings and a big stage up front. There were many tables, some of them covered, so he knew the place had gaming.

As he approached the bar several men standing there turned to eye him, as the bartender walked his way.

"What can I get for you, my friend?" the big man asked, with a slight accent. If Clint hadn't been in The Dutchman Saloon in a town called Little Amsterdam, he would have mistaken the man's accent for German.

Minnesota was cool. Having washed his face he felt fairly refreshed.

With boarding taken care of for himself and Eclipse, his next step was a meal.

***

Once again he didn't ask anyone to recommend a restaurant, but rather made the choice himself.

He walked by several places and finally chose one he thought looked, well, Dutch. And this was where he saw the second thing about Minnesota that impressed him.

She was in her 20's, waiting tables, wearing an outfit that made her look like a milk maid, but it was cinched at the waist, so that her generous breasts were accented. The white top left her shoulders and a very small, shadowy and mysterious bit of a cleft between her breasts visible. At the moment she was carrying four plates filled with meat and potatoes, wearing a wide, beautiful smile on her face. Her hair was so blonde it almost looked white and hung down to just barely brush the pale skin of her shoulders.

It wasn't yet supper time, but the restaurant was doing a decent business. A man approached him with a smile. He had white hair and pink skin.

"Yes, sir?" he said.

"A table, please."

"Will you be eating with anyone else?" the man asked, in that slight accent Clint had been hearing around town.

"No, just me."

"A table by the window, then?"

"No, thank you," Clint said, "one as far from the window as possible."

"As you wish, sir." He turned and yelled "Gerta!" and the girl Clint had been admiring turned and looked at him.

"Yes, Poppa?"

"Please take this gentleman to a back table. He will be eating alone."

"Yes, Poppa." She rushed over to Clint and treated him to that smile. "Follow me, please."

"My pleasure."

It was indeed a pleasure to walk behind this solidly built girl.

Chapter Three

The food was excellent, but it was hard for Clint to concentrate on it with the girl, Gerta, darting about the room, waiting on the other diners, smiling and laughing.

Her father seemed to just loiter by the front door, his arms crossed, watching his daughter intently. Clint wondered if there was another family member in the kitchen, doing the cooking.

"Can I get anything else for you, sir?" Gerta asked him, stopping by his table.

"You can give my compliments to your cook, whoever that is," he said.

She laughed. "That is Momma, and she will be very happy to hear it. More coffee?"

"Please. I don't think I've ever had coffee like this. It has a fruity, almost chocolate aftertaste."

"That is our Dutch coffee," she told him. "We brew it using cold water, not hot. It brings out hidden flavors in the beans."

She took his plate away, came back with a pot of coffee.

"And desert? Some Chipolata? Or Spekkoek?"

"What are those?"

"Chipolata is a fresh fruit pudding, and the Spekkoek is a spice cake."

"What do you recommend?"

She studied him for a moment, then said, "I believe you are a cake man."

"All right, then," he said, "the spice cake."

"Wise choice," she said, giving him a wink.

As she turned and went back to the kitchen Clint could see her father glowering at him. The girl had an open and friendly face and manner, but Clint couldn't help having bawdy thoughts when she winked at him. Maybe her father was reading his mind.

She brought the cake, which was a perfect finish to the Dutch meal he'd consumed. The crowd had thinned out, so Gerta came by his table again.

"Anything else, sir?" she asked.

"Yes," he said, "you have to stop calling me sir. My name's Clint."

"Well, Clint," she said, "if you come back again, I will remember that."

"Oh, I think I'll be back," he said.

"So you are not just passing through?" she asked.

"I was," he said, "but I think I might be changing my mind."

"So our food has brought about this change of heart?" she asked.

"Sure," he said, "let's say it's the food."

She blushed as he handed her the money for the meal, and their hands lingered.

"Gerta!" her father snapped from the door. "You have other customers."

"Yes, Poppa," she said, and then whispered to Clint, "but none as handsome."

She hurried to the other tables; Clint rose and walked to the door.

"An excellent meal," he told Gerta's father.

"All of our food is excellent," the man said, with a hard stare. "My wife is a wonderful cook."

"Yes, she is. I sent her my compliments with your daughter."

"Yes," the man said, "My daughter—a sweet and innocent girl."

"Yes," Clint said, getting the message loud and clear, "yes, she is."

He went outside.

***

Clint took a stroll to walk off the heavy meal he'd had. He saw that the town had more than just a Dutch theme. It was a decidedly Dutch community, and he wondered who had brought that influence to this part of Minnesota.

He decided to take the question to someone who was very likely to be a town historian—a bartender. He went back to the Dutchman Saloon, where he had been greeted so warmly when he first arrived.

"Ah, you are back!" the bartender said, happily.

The saloon was doing more business than it had been before, but there was still plenty of room at the bar for Clint.

"Yes, I am," Clint said. "I'd like another of those cold beers."

"Of course, my friend," the bartender said. "This one will be on me, eh?"

"Thanks."

As Clint drank, the bartender folded his arms and watched him.

"So, what do you think of our community now that you have seen some of it?"

"It's very nice," Clint said. "Quiet and peaceful."

"Indeed it is."

"Do you have a sheriff or marshal?" Clint asked.

"We have a High Commissioner," the man said, proudly.

"Really?" Clint said. "Is he like a sheriff, or a chief of police?"

"Back home in the Netherlands he would be referred to as a Chief Commissioner, but here we have slightly changed it. We are, after all, in a new place."

"So many of you have actually come here from the Netherlands?"

"Gustav and Hildegard came here from New York to start our community," the man said.

"Gustav?"

"Gustav Vanderhoff and his wife Hildegard, yes," the bartender said. "They wanted to open the West to our people, and have brought all of us here, together."

"Well," Clint said, "it looks like that's exactly what they've done, opened up the West to you."

"I came here from Philadelphia, but many of us came directly from the Netherlands."

"So is Mr. Vanderhoff the Mayor?"

"He has a big ranch outside of town," the bartender said. "He is not the mayor, he is simply our founder. And he named the town."

Clint was impressed that such a man would not have named the town after himself and appointed himself mayor.

"Sounds like an impressive man," Clint commented.

"Yes, he is," the bartender said, "and so is his wife. You should meet them while you are here."

"Maybe I will," Clint said. "They ever come in here?"

"Gustav does," the man said, "Occasionally. Not Hilda. She has become a homebody."

The bartender moved on down the bar to serve others, and Clint turned with his beer in hand and putting his back to the bar.

Chapter Four

The naked woman could not turn her eyes away from the man's huge erection. It stuck out from a dark tangle of hair like an oak tree from a clump of bushes.

"Hurry," she urged him. "I don't have much time."

As she lay back on the hay bed and spread her legs for him he straddled her, driving that monstrous penis into her juicy pussy. Briefly, he ravaged her overly large breasts, but soon he was involved in his own sensations.

"Oh, yes!" she gasped, her eyes going wide.

She had wide hips, and an ample bottom that absorbed the impact of his thrusts. She wrapped her legs around his waist and her arms around his torso, hanging on for dear life as he pounded her. She knew he was only seeking his own relief, but she didn't care. In that moment this what was she wanted, a quick poke in the hay before she had to go back into the house to her husband.

This was not the first of her husband's ranch hands she had done this with. And she didn't care if they talked about it among themselves afterward. If ten men went to her husband and told her that they had been with her, he would not have believed any one of them. That was how much he loved and believed in her.

After the first man she had felt a twinge of guilt, but now, after this one, there would be nothing but great satisfaction. She had purposely picked this giant of a man because she knew there would be no questions asked, and no professions of love afterward. This was just what it was, quite literally, a roll in the hay, to be forgotten when it was over.

Forgotten, that is, until the next time.

She saw the man open his mouth to roar as he exploded into her, and she hastily clamped both of her hands over his mouth. She muffled his cries until he was finished pumping into her and rolled off.

Her own release had not come, but she could take care of that later, as she played this encounter back to herself in her mind in a bath. Of all the men she had been with, including her husband, none of them had brought her to her own passionate ending. For years that had been something she had only been able to accomplish by herself. But she knew this was part of the reason for her many dalliances. She would have loved to come across a man who could satisfy her, completely.

And when that did finally happen, she had no idea what would come after . . .

***

When she entered the house, the front of her dress smoothed down, her hair rearranged and carefully inspected for any strands of hay, her husband asked, "Hilda, where have you been?"

"Tending my garden," she said. "There was much weeding to be done."

He embraced her. She always wondered when he did that if he didn't smell the sex on her or didn't care.

"I missed you."

She pushed him away. "You're a crazy old man, Gustav."

At sixty he was twenty years her senior, with hair the color of steel, a thick chest and a thickening waist. He was still a viral man, got out to work his ranch with his men almost every day, but in bed he was . . . well, just woeful. If it wasn't for his money, and the fact that he had brought her there from the Netherlands, she probably would have left him years ago. But now she was comforted by the things he did do for her and found the things he couldn't do elsewhere.

"And you smell like a horse," she said, laughing.

"Yes, I have been working with the stock, my love," he said. "But I will clean up for supper."

"And I will go and talk with Anneke and see what she is preparing for our meal."

He blew her a kiss and walked out the front door. She shook her head and decided to wash the scent of the ranch hand off of her before talking to the cook. Anneke's sense of smell was not as useless as her husband's.

Chapter Five

Clint felt a tap on his shoulder, turned to find the bartender looking at him.

"There's somebody you should meet," he said. "Just comin' in the front doors, now."

Clint looked, saw a thickset man, just under six feet, enter and return a few waves from customers. Then he turned and walked to the bar.

"Karl," he said, "A beer, please."

"Yes, sir." He leaned close to Clint and whispered, "The High Commissioner."

The lawman in town seemed to be in his 50s, with a square jaw, wide shoulders, a shirt and jeans with no gunbelt on his waist, and a hat almost like the kind the captain of a ship would wear. Clint assumed this was a Dutch hat.

"Commissioner," Karl the bartender said as he delivered the man's beer, "we have a stranger in our town."

"I heard that," the man said, "but I have not heard much about him."

"Well, he's right here," Karl said, indicating Clint. "I told him he should meet you."

"Then make the introduction, Karl," the lawman said, turning to face Clint.

"High Commissioner Abraham De Jong, meet . . . you know, I never asked your name," Karl said.

"No, you didn't," Clint said. He faced the commissioner. "I'm Clint Adams."

The commissioner was about to extend his hand to shake when he suddenly stopped and drew it back, slowly.

"The Gunsmith?" he asked.

Karl looked shocked.

"That's right."

"What brings you to Little Amsterdam, Mr. Adams?" the commissioner asked.

"I was just riding, saw the town sign and was curious," Clint said.

"So you have no business here?"

"Not at all," Clint said. "I never heard of the town until earlier today."

"And how long do you intend to stay?" "Well, I guess that depends on whether or not you're going to order me to leave."

"I would not do that," the commissioner said. "You have done nothing wrong, here . . . that I know of."

"I haven't done a thing except ride in," Clint said.

"Did you think no one here would know who you are?" the commissioner asked.

"I can't ever worry about that, Commissioner," Clint said. "If I did, I'd never be able to ride into any town."

"But we're Dutch here," the commissioner said, "and this is Minnesota, not the Southwest. Perhaps you thought we would never have heard of you?"

"No," Clint said. "You've lived in this country long enough to have heard of me."

"Do you think you can go anywhere anonymously?" the commissioner asked.

"Maybe."

"Where?"

"The Netherlands?"

Commissioner DeJong laughed at that, and Karl joined in, nervously.

"Oh, relax, Karl," the commissioner said. "Mr. Adams is our guest. We must treat him like one."

"Yes, sir," Karl said. "I was just telling him he should meet Gustav and Hilda."

"Ah," the commissioner said, "our illustrious founder and his wife. Very interesting people." He finished his beer and put the empty mug on the bar. "Hilda will like you. Goodnight."

"Good-night, Commissioner."

As the lawman left, Clint turned to Karl, who was now looking at him, nervously.

"Relax, Karl," he said, "I'm not going to shoot you."

"Oh," Karl said, with a fake smile, "I wasn't worried . . ."

"What did he mean when he said Hilda will like me?" Clint asked.

"Hilda likes men."

"Does her husband know?"

"He either doesn't," Karl said, "or he pretends he doesn't."

"But a lot of people do know?"

"Yes," Karl said. "Some of the ranch hands come here and talk."

"That's too bad," Clint said. "The man should be getting respect."

"He is respected," Karl assured Clint, "that is why nobody tells him."

Chapter Six

Clint's first night in Little Amsterdam was peaceful and quiet. He came down the next morning and had breakfast in the small hotel dining room. The food was good, but not as good as it had been the night before.

The waiter suggested and brought him *uitsmijter*; slices of bread topped with fried eggs, ham and cheese. He ate it all hungrily, washed it down with good strong coffee.

"How was that?" the waiter asked.

"Delicious," he said. "I had my first Dutch food last night, and now this was my first Dutch breakfast. I could get used to this."

"You come back anytime, sir," the waiter said. "There is a lot more where this came from."

"Don't worry," Clint said. "I'll be eating a lot more while I'm here."

"Yes, sir."

The waiter accepted Clint's payment, and turned to leave.

"Before you go . . ."

"Yes, sir?"

". . . can you tell me anything about the people who founded this place. What was it? Gustav and . . ."

". . . Hilda," the waiter said. "Gustav and Hilda. Actually, it was Gustav. He came here, started building, named the place, and then as other people moved in they built more of it."

"What kind of people are they?"

"Good people," the waiter said. "If they weren't, I would not have come here all the way from the Netherlands."

"And you're glad you did?" Clint asked.

"Very glad."

"I've, uh, heard some rumors about them," Clint said, "about their . . . relationship?"

"I do not believe rumors," the waiter said "I pay no attention to them. Gustav is a good man, and Hilda is . . . a nice lady. Can I do anything else for you?"

"Yes," Clint said, "can you tell me where their ranch is?"

***

Clint didn't know why, but he wanted to meet Gustav and Hilda Vanderhoff. He also wanted to take Eclipse out for a ride. He didn't know how long he was going to stay in Little Amsterdam, but he wanted to find out more about it, himself. And if he was going to be in town a while, Eclipse needed to exercise from time to time. Even though they had ridden in off the trail only yesterday. The big guy liked to stretch his legs.

***

He rode out of Little Amsterdam and followed the directions the waiter had given him. The ranch was about a half hour north of town. When he came within sight of it he reined in and took a look.

The house had been built on a hill, and the rest of it—the barn, the corral, and bunkhouse—all around it. There were half a dozen horses in the corral, and a few men milling about them. He thought about riding in, but how would he explain his curiosity?

Maybe that's all he had to say, that he was curious. He wondered if all the ranch hands were also Dutch, or if Gustav had hired some legitimate hands?

He heard somebody riding up behind him and decided to just take it as it came.

"Can I help you?" a man called.

He turned in his saddle to look at the man who was approaching, astride a good looking Appaloosa that wore a brand of a G with a bar underneath it. The Bar G.

"Just having a look," Clint said.

"Why?" the man asked. He reined in while he was still five or six feet away. He had a gun on his hip, and a rifle in a scabbard.

"I've never seen a ranch house built up on a hill like that before," Clint said, truthfully.

"The owner comes from meager beginnings," the man said, "or, at least, that's what he says. He says he wants to look down at what he owns."

"I can see that," Clint said. "What kind of a guy is he?"

"He's a good man. Founded a town that's not too far from here."

"Little Amsterdam?"

"That's the one."

"So he owns this ranch, and the town?"

"He doesn't own the town," the man said. "He built it, and named it, but he don't own it. He says the people who live and work in town should own it."

"So he gave it to them?"

"That's about it."

"He sounds like a special kind of man."

"He is. Now, before I tell you any more, just who are you?" the man asked.

"Are you law?" Clint asked.

"My name's Rance Edwards. I'm the foreman here," the man said. "I was out checking some fence, saw you sittin' here."

"Little Amsterdam's Dutch, isn't it?"

"That's right."

"And the man who owns this ranch?"

"Also Dutch."

"But you're not."

"No," he said, "I'm good old red blooded American. He wanted somebody runnin' the ranch who knew what they were doin'."

"I get that."

"Who are you, Mister?"

"My name's Adams," he replied, "Clint Adams."

Edwards shifted in his saddle.

"The Gunsmith?"

"That's right."

"And you were just ridin' by?"

"I'm staying in town, took my horse out for some exercise," Clint said.

"Why are you in town?"

"I was riding near here, saw that sign with the town's name on it, got curious."

"That's all it was? Curiosity?"

"That's it," Clint said, with a shrug.

"What would you say to meetin' Mr. Vanderhoff? Gustav, the owner?"

"I'd say why not? How often will I get to meet such a man?"

"Not often," Edwards said. "Come on, let's ride in."

Chapter Seven

Clint followed the foreman down to the ranch. They attracted the attention of the hands as they rode up to the foot of the hill the house was on. It was even steeper than Clint had first thought. A wooden staircase had been built into the side of the hill, leading to a front porch and door.

"Lemme tell the boss you're here," Edwards said. "I'm sure he'll wanna meet you."

"Okay."

"You want your horse looked after?"

"I don't expect to be here that long," Clint said. "He's fine right here."

"Beautiful animal," Edwards said. "You better tie him off."

"Don't worry," Clint said, "he won't go anywhere."

"Suit yerself."

Rance Edwards went up the steps to the front door of the house and entered without knocking. Some of the hands came closer to get a better look at Eclipse, studying Clint at the same time.

"Howdy," Clint said.

They all nodded, but nobody spoke. They seemed like ranch hands, none of them were armed. Normally, there was no reason for a ranch hand to wear a gun when he was on the job—unless the ranch happened to be in Indian territory.

Finally, one man spoke.

"That's some good lookin' animal."

"Thanks," Clint said.

"Wouldn't be lookin' to sell, would ya?" another man asked.

"Nope."

"Is he fast?"

"Fast, and he's got stamina."

"Mind if we look 'im over?"

"Just be warned," Clint said dismounting, "he doesn't like to be touched by strangers. He might take off a finger."

"I'll take that chance," the first man said.

He approached Eclipse, reached out to stroke his neck, and the Darley Arabian turned his head and snapped, barely missing a finger.

"Whoa!" somebody said, as the man pulled his hand back, and his colleagues laughed.

"I warned you," Clint said.

"You gonna tie him off?" another man asked.

Clint told the man the same thing he told Edwards, the foreman.

"He's not going anywhere," Clint said. "He'll stand right here until I get back."

"He's that well trained?"

"He's that smart," Clint said.

"What if one of us tries to ride 'im?" the first man said, still cradling the finger he'd almost lost.

"He'll throw you, and then stomp you."

"So he's a killer?"

"Not a killer," Clint said, "just particular about who rides him."

The front door of the house opened, and the foreman stepped out.

"You men get back to work!" he shouted.

"Sure, boss," somebody said, and they scattered.

"Come on up, Mr. Adams."

Clint took the steps up to the porch and stood alongside the foreman, looking out at the property.

"Sorry about that," he told Clint. "The men enjoy good horseflesh."

"I can see why he wants to look out from up here," Clint said.

"Mr. Vanderhoff is excited to meet you," Edwards said. "Come on in."

Chapter Eight

The house was well built, sturdy, and not ostentatious like some ranch houses Clint had seen lately. There was the good smell of Dutch food inside.

"The men get Dutch food in the mess?" Clint asked.

"Some days," Edwards said.

"How many of the hands are Dutch?"

"A few. When we hired I had to take men who knew the job. We took some who needed to be trained. This way."

It was a short walk to a living room with a wooden floor, homemade furniture, a large desk in front of a front window. Across from the desk was a large stone fireplace, and in the back, a staircase to the second floor.

There was a man standing next to the sofa who looked as sturdy as the house was. He was widely built, not over six feet, but seemed even shorter because of his girth. His hair was steel grey, but there was a lot of it, and his face was weathered, with deep lines that looked like cracks.

"Mr. Adams?" he said. "I am Gustav Vanderhoff."

"Mr. Vanderhoff," Clint said. "Thanks for seeing me."

"Well, when Rance told me that you were admiring the house, I thought I would take advantage of the chance to show it off."

"Gustav pretty much built this place single-handed," Rance Edwards said.

"Not at all," Gustav said. "I had some help." He had the heaviest Dutch accent Clint had heard since he was in town. It sounded like he said, "Nawt et awl."

"Would you like a drink?"

"Do you have something Dutch?" Clint asked. "I've been enjoying your Dutch food since I got to town."

"We have some Genever," Gustav said, pronouncing it Yen-ae-ver.

"Excellent. Rance, you, too?"

"Not me," the foreman said. "I hate that stuff!"

Gustav went to a sideboard next to the fireplace, poured two shot glasses of clear liquid from a decanter. He walked across the room and handed it to Clint.

"First sip a bit off the top," Gustav instructed, "and then toss off the rest. Like this." He demonstrated, smacked his lips afterward.

Clint sipped a bit of it off the top, mostly just wetting his lips, and then tossed off the rest. It burned going down, but it reminded him very much of the one time he had tried gin.

"What do you think?" Gustav asked.

"Interesting," Clint said, "but my beverages of choice are beer, and coffee."

"Ah, then you have had the beer at the Dutchman?"

"Yes," Clint said, "I got here yesterday and found that place. It was very good."

"Have a seat," Gustav said. "We will have coffee and talk. Rance, go to the kitchen and tell Mama to bring coffee."

"Mama?" Clint said. "Did you bring your mother over from the Netherlands?"

"No, no," Gustav said, as they sat, "she is not my mother, and before you ask, I do not call my wife Mama. But Mama, she cooks for us, and this is what we call her."

"I see."

"So tell me, Mr. Adams—"

"Please, call me Clint."

"Clint . . . what really brought you to this part of the country?"

"I was in Nebraska, near the border, and I admit, I don't know that much about Minnesota. I've been here once or twice, but not enough to know it well. So I thought I'd ride up. I crossed the border, saw the sign for Little Amsterdam, and was curious. I've been to New York, and know it was once settled by the Dutch, who called it New Amsterdam." He spread his hands. "So I rode here."

"Uh-huh," Gustav said, not seeming very convinced. "You will forgive me, but you are a man of reputation. I did not know men such as you simply . . . wandered."

"And why not?"

"Forgive me," Gustav said, "but when I came to this country I read of men such as you. It seemed you always had somewhere to go, something to do, someone to . . . uh . . ."

"Kill?"

"Well, yes."

"You must have spent time in the East, and read dime novels," Clint said.

"That is true, but also newspaper accounts."

"I try to stay out of the newspapers."

"But you were in Dodge City," Gustav said, "and Tombstone, and such places."

"I left Tombstone before the commotion there," Clint said. "I was in Dodge during the rowdy days, but I was part of a group of men who kept the peace."

"Then obviously I am misinformed," Gustav said, "and I must apologize."

At that point a woman came down the stairs. She stopped at a landing before proceeding the rest of the way, and stood there, as if she wanted Clint to take a long look.

So he did.

Chapter Nine

The first thing he noticed was that she was younger than her husband. Maybe that was why there were rumors about the men she'd been with.

She was a good-looking woman, tall and blonde with pale skin, wide hips and a full thrust of breasts that she did not dress to hide. He wondered if this was a prime example of what Dutch women looked like?

"My dear," Gustav said, "we have a guest."

"So I heard," she said, coming down the rest of the way.

"This is Clint Adams," Gustav said, as his wife approached them. "Mr. Adams, this is Hildegard."

"I'm very happy to meet you, Mr. Adams," she said, shaking his hand. She had a cool, strong grip. "Are you doing business with my husband?"

"No, Ma'am," Clint said, "I was just riding past and wanted to have a closer look at the house on the hill."

"Oh, yeah," Hildegard said, "my husband does like to look down on his holdings, doesn't he?"

"I asked Anneke to make some coffee, Hilda," Gustav said. "Could you check and see if she is ready for us?"

"Of course, my dear." She leaned over and kissed her husband's cheek, but all the while she was looking at Clint.

"Lovely woman," Clint commented.

"Yes, she is." Gustav was staring after his wife, until she was out of sight.

"Is she happy here?"

Now Gustav looked at Clint.

"Why would you ask that?"

"A lot of women who came west from the east aren't happy in the wilderness," Clint said. "You and your wife came from much further away than that."

"She is happy," Gustav said. "The place where she was unhappy was back home—although now, this is home, so I should not put it that way."

"My love?" His wife appeared in the doorway, again. "The coffee is ready."

"Good," Gustav said, "we'll have it on the dining room table and continue to get to know each other . . . better. Come."

Clint allowed himself to be ushered into the dining room, where cups and saucers and a large pot of coffee had been put out.

Gustav sat at the head of the table, with Hildegard at the other end. Clint sat between them. Anneke turned out to be a white-haired old lady who looked like everybody's mother. She came and poured the coffee for all of them.

"Thank you," Clint said. "It smells wonderful."

"Yes, thank you, Anneke," Hilda said. "You can go back to the kitchen, now."

Clint caught the look Anneke gave Hildegard. The two women obviously didn't like each other.

"How long do you intend to stay in Amsterdam, Mr. Adams?" Hilda asked. Her accent was not as thick as her husband's.

"I'm not sure," Clint said. "I got here, and it's a very nice town."

"That it is," she agreed. "It's certainly worth your while to stay around and see more of it . . . experience more."

"I agree," Gustav said, "you must stay. And you can be our guest here."

"That's a wonderful idea."

"No, no," Clint said, "I'm fine in the hotel."

"You don't like our house?" Hilda asked.

"It's not that," he said. "A man like me, with my reputation, tends to attract trouble. I wouldn't want to bring that into your head."

"Very considerate of you," Gustav commented.

"But do you really think Mr. Adams is going to have trouble in Little Amsterdam?" Hilda asked. "It is a paradise." She looked at Clint. "And what reputation are you speaking of?"

"Hilda," Gustav said, "Mr. Adams is also known as the Gunsmith."

She put her hand over her mouth.

"I am so sorry," she said, "I did not realize."

"It's okay. Sometimes I'd just as soon people don't recognize my name."

"But . . . does that happen?" Gustav asked. "Everywhere?"

"No," Clint said, "but frequently."

"So then men are always trying to kill you," Gustav said.

"Pretty much."

"But what a terrible way to live," Hilda said. "Isn't there something you can do? Perhaps . . . settle down. Oh, I did not ask if you are married."

"Never have been. And I've thought about settling down, but I think it's too late. I'd just attract trouble to whatever community I decided to settle in."

"You are very concerned about someone else getting hurt because of you, aren't you?" Hilda asked.

"Yes, I am," Clint said. "I'd rather not be responsible for the deaths of innocent people."

"You are a very good man," Hilda said.

"How is the coffee?" Gustav asked.

"It's very good," Clint said. "Everything I've had since I got to town has been delicious."

"And I have enjoyed everything American that I have had since we moved here," Hilda said, staring at Clint.

Having heard the rumors about her made Clint wonder exactly what she was referring to.

Chapter Ten

During coffee Clint heard about Gustav's dream to come to the United States.

"He heard all those stories about the streets paved with gold," Hilda said, "and he convinced me that was what we would find when we got here. Then we disembarked from the ship in New York harbor . . ." She shook her head. Obviously, the memory was not a good one.

"Hilda was a little disappointed to find that roads were not literally gold," Gustav said, "but I saw the possibilities."

"And is that what brought you here?" Clint asked. "Possibilities?"

"I met a man who came from Minnesota," Gustav said. "He was living in New York, but he missed his home so much. He talked about the land, the weather, the wolves . . . everything he recalled from his childhood. I thought this sounded like a good place to bring a family and raise them."

"So he brought us here, built the town, built this house and we made it our home." Listening to her tone of voice, it didn't sound like a good thing.

"I made Little Amsterdam available to any Dutch family who wanted to come here and make a contribution."

"Contributions like the candy store, the tea shop, the shoe store?"

"Exactly," Gustav said. "The kind of places you never saw in Dodge City and Abilene. I did not come west to be a cowboy, and neither did the people who followed me."

"And yet here we are, on your ranch."

"Exactly," Hilda said. "My Gustav actually is becoming a cowboy."

"We had to have a way to make a living," Gustav argued. "Raising horses is something I enjoy very much. My father had horses when I was a child. This just seemed natural to me."

"So far I have been able to keep him from wearing a gun," Hilda said, "but I don't know how much longer I can do that."

"I am not a gunfighter," Gustav said, "and I will never be . . . but it occurs to me that to live here a man must know how to defend himself, and his family.

"That's true."

"Perhaps while you are here," Gustav said, "you might be able to give me some shooting lessons."

Clint looked at Hilda, who rolled her eyes.

"Sure," he said to Gustav, "I'd be happy to, but right now I better get going. My horse has been out front all this time."

"Come," Gustav said, rising, "I will walk you out."

***

When they came down the stairs Gustav was amazed by Eclipse. From the porch Hilda watched them both descend.

"What an amazing animal!" Gustav praised, walking around Eclipse, knowing enough not to try to touch him. "I will bet he has speed as well as stamina."

"Exactly."

"Did you raise him?"

"I'm afraid not," Clint said. "He was a gift."

"He is a Darley Arabian, is he not?"

"You know your horseflesh."

"But I know nothing about that," Gustav said, indicating the sidearm in Clint's holster. "Do you work on them, yourself?"

"I do," Clint said. "The Gunsmith isn't just a reputation, it's something that I am. For a while I rode around in a wagon, working on people's guns."

"I would like to learn that, as well as how to shoot them," Gustav said.

"Learning to shoot a gun won't be hard," Clint said. "It's making sure you hit what you point at. Then learning to take them apart and put them back together again, that will just take time."

"I will come and see you at the hotel," Gustav said.

"Sure thing," Clint said. "When you're ready, we can get started."

"And I will pay you for your time."

"Absolutely not," Clint said, mounting up.

"Well, then," Gustav said, "I will see you are not charged for your room, or any of your meals and drinks."

"Gustav," Clint said, "the people in town are trying to make a living, too. I'll pay for everything I get or use, and I'll teach you to shoot as a favor for a new friend."

"Very well, then," Gustav said, putting his hand out, "my new friend."

Clint reached down, shook the man's hand, then turned Eclipse to leave. He saw Hilda watching him from the porch, and the ranch hands watching from the corral.

As he rode out he was thinking two things. First, he always found it interesting to teach someone to shoot. A lot depended on how natural their ability was.

The second thing that occurred to him was that Gustav Vanderhoff and the town he had built seemed to be too good to be true.

Chapter Eleven

By the next morning Clint's curiosity had eaten a hole in his sensibility.

He thought about it all night and was convinced that something was going on in Little Amsterdam. It seemed a nice, peaceful town, he could leave it at that and keep traveling. But something niggled at him all night long, keeping him from sleeping soundly.

He came down to the hotel dining room early, asked the waiter if he could get a good old American breakfast of steak-and-eggs.

"Well, sure, Mr. Adams," the man said. "You can get whatever you want."

"Thanks."

"Coffee?"

"Yep."

"Dutch or American?" the man asked.

"Let's go American with that too, today."

So far he'd been charmed by the all of the Dutch people, the Dutch food, and the young Dutch girl working in the other restaurant.

Last night Gustav and Hilda also turned the charm on for him, and now he had a deal with Gustav to teach him how to shoot. And if the stories about Hilda were true, she probably had her own plans for him, as well. He thought having some

American food and coffee would give him time to think with a clear head.

The cook was apparently as good with American food as he was with Dutch. The steak-and-eggs were perfect, as were the hot biscuits they served with it. And the coffee he washed it all down with was black and strong.

"Say, what goes on around here?" he asked, the waiter, as he poured more coffee.

"What do you mean, sir?" the man asked, frowning down at him.

"You know, for fun," Clint said. "What do people do? Is there any gambling?"

For a moment, the waiter looked very uncomfortable with the question.

"I guess . . . folks in this town don't do much for fun," he finally said. "We're all working to make Little Amsterdam a happy and pleasant place to live."

"I see. So no gambling?"

"Not that I know of, sir," the waiter said, "I mean, we have saloons, of course, but I've never heard of gambling in any of them."

"Uh-huh. Okay, thanks."

"If you want," the waiter said, "we can put the cost of the breakfast on your hotel bill. You can pay the whole thing when you check out."

"Okay, let's do that."

"Yes, sir."

Clint put something on the table for the waiter and then left the dining room and the hotel.

Whether the town had gambling or not, it did have saloons, as the waiter had said, which meant it had bartenders. And bartenders knew everything. But the bartender Clint had spoken to already was Dutch. There had to be some people in town, as there were on Gustav's ranch, who weren't Dutch. And maybe one of them was a bartender.

But it was early, too early for saloons to be opened in a town like this. Clint decided to find out if any of the other businesses—feed and grain, for instance, or the livery stable— were run by folks who weren't Dutch. And perhaps they'd be the talkative type.

So he took a turn around town, stopped in some of the stores—a leather shop and a gun shop—but he didn't find shopkeepers who weren't Dutch. And the ones he did talk to echoed the waiter's sentiments.

"We are all working to make Little Amsterdam a happy and pleasant place to live."

It was as if they had all been rehearsed to say that if anyone ever asked.

***

As it got later in the afternoon the saloons began to open. Clint started stopping into them, having a beer and making conversation with the bartenders, and others at the bar. He left the first saloon he had stopped in the day before, the Dutch- man, for last.

The bartenders were talkative, as usual, but when it came to Little Amsterdam and what its aim was, they all had exactly the same damn line about it being a happy and pleasant place to live.

Except one.

Clint found a small saloon on a side street. There was nothing fancy about it, right down to the board that had been nailed above the front entrance, with THE BOTTOM SALOON written on it.

With real interest, he went through the batwing doors, not knowing what to expect.

Chapter Twelve

The inside of The Bottom was a mixture of mismatched tables and chairs, broken light fixtures, dirty floors and overflowing spittoons. He approached the bar, stopped himself just before leaning his elbows on it, as it looked sticky.

"You in the right place, friend?" the burly, dour-faced bartender asked.

"You got beer?"

"Yeah, we got beer."

"Then I'm in the right place. Let me have one."

The bartender brought a mug up from beneath the bar, blew in it, and then filled and set it down in front of Clint.

"Four bits."

"That's steep."

"It's the ambience," the man said.

Clint laughed at that and paid the man. At the end of the bar one saloon girl stared, looking him over. She had dark black hair, pale skin and was wearing a red dress that showed a lot of shoulder and breast. She was the cleanest thing in the place.

"The ambience seems pretty good to me," Clint said.

The bartender looked at the other end of the bar.

"That's Miley," he said.

"I'll bet."

"You interested in spending time with her?"

"Not just now." Clint stared down at the beer, wondered how much dirt he'd get when he drank it. But if he wanted the man to talk to him, he figured he'd at least better take a sip.

He picked it up, sipped it and set it down. The dirt intake wasn't too bad—certainly less than riding on the trail during a sand storm.

"This is an odd little town," he commented.

"You don't know the half of it," the bartender said, which made Clint happy. He may just have come to the right place.

"Really?" Clint asked. "How so?"

"Dutchies all over the place."

"Well," Clint said, "I assumed the town was Dutch from the name."

"You knew more than me, then," the man said. "I came here, opened the place, and then tried to get customers. But because I ain't a Dutchy, they don't come here."

Clint looked around. There were two men leaning on the bar between him and Miley, and a few more seated at rickety tables.

"Looks like you've got customers."

"They ain't Dutchies," the bartender said, "and, believe it or not, this is a busy night for me."

"Why so many Dutch, then?" Clint asked. "What are they trying to build here?"

"Beats me," he said. "Everybody's got the same story."

"They want to work to make it a 'happy and pleasant place to live?' That the one you're talking about?"

"That's the one," the man said.

"Sure seems like they learned it real well," Clint commented.

"And get this," the man said. "They won't let me have gamblin' here."

"Why do you stay?" Clint asked.

"I spent the last of my money buyin' this place," the bartender said, "and I ain't makin' it in handfuls. But when I do get enough, or find a buyer, I'm gone."

Clint looked down at the girl.

"What about Miley?"

"She comes with the place," he said.

"She was here when you got here?"

"No, I hired her, but I don't expect her to go with me when I leave," he said. "I mean, look at her and look at me."

Clint saw what he meant. He took another sip of beer.

"How long you stayin' in town?" the bartender asked.

"I don't know," Clint said. "I had no plans when I got here. I just saw the name on the road and thought I'd take a look."

"How d'ya feel about Dutchies?"

"I've got no problem with them."

"Then you'll probably be all right, here," the bartender said.

"I like the name of this place," Clint said. "What's your name?"

I'm Frank Kelton." He put his hand out to shake.

"Clint Adams," Clint said, shaking the hand.

"What the hell are you doin' here?" Kelton asked, his eyes wide. It was the first time the dour expression had left his face.

It made him look ten years younger than the fifty Clint had him figured for.

"If I knew the Gunsmith was comin' to my place," Kelton went on, "I mighta cleaned up. Here." He grabbed Clint's beer. "Lemme get ya a clean glass."

"Much obliged."

He went to the other end of the bar for the clean glass, said something to Miley, then came back with the glass full.

"There ya go."

"Thank you, Mr. Kelton."

"Oh, hey, just call me Frank."

"And you call me Clint," he said. "And now that we're on a first name basis, let's really talk."

Chapter Thirteen

"Talk about what?" Frank Kelton asked.

"This place," Clint said. "This town."

"What about it?"

"It's just too good to be true," Clint said. "There's got to be something going on here."

"To tell you the truth," Kelton said, "I've felt the same way for a while, but I can't see what it is."

"Well, like you say," Clint replied, "the Dutch don't come in here. Do any of your customers have any information? I mean, they must have some dealings with the Dutch storekeepers. And what about Miley?" He looked down the bar, but the girl was gone. "Does she spend any time with any Dutch men?"

"You'd have to ask her, but if she does she ain't meetin' 'em here."

"Maybe I'll talk to her, when she comes back."

"Nobody's ever said anythin'," Kelton said, "but I could ask."

"I'd appreciate that."

"But, if you don't mind me askin', why?"

"Curiosity, plain and simple," Clint said.

"So you ain't lookin' for somebody here?" Kelton asked. "Ain't on a job of some kind?"

"Nothing like that," Clint said. "I rode in, met some people, I even met Gustav and his wife."

"Wow, I ain't even met 'em," Kelton said. "They don't come to town all that much."

"Is that a fact?"

"Well, he don't," Kelton amended. "Rumor is she comes from time to time."

"I heard those rumors."

"I know a couple of ranch hands from the Gustav spread who claim they ain't just rumors," Kelton said. "They say they been with her."

"What else do they say?"

"That she almost killed 'em," Kelton said. "They say she's an animal in bed—or on a hay bale, or the ground. Wherever."

"And Gustav doesn't know?"

"Oh, he's gotta know," Kelton said. "My bet is, he don't much care."

"But it's his wife."

"You met 'em," Kelton said. "You seen the difference in age?"

"I have, yes," Clint said. "She's got to be twenty years younger."

"And hungrier, if ya know what I mean."

"I think I do." Clint finished the beer in the clean glass the bartender had given him. "Listen, Frank, I'd appreciate anything you can find out for me. My problem with curiosity is that it eats at me."

"I get it," Kelton said. "Come on back, Clint, and I'll keep a clean glass for ya."

"I appreciate that."

He left the Bottom Saloon but before he could get far somebody hissed at him from the alley next to it.

"Hey!"

He turned and saw the girl, Miley, looking out at him.

"Hello."

"Get in here before somebody sees us!" she said, urgently.

She backed up and he entered the alley with her.

"What's going on?"

"It sounds like you have a lot of questions," she said.

This close the girl looked all of twenty-five, and she not only looked clean, she smelled it—clean and fresh, still wearing her red dress. She had a lovely, long neck, and full breasts that swelled above her dress, threatening to leap out.

"I do have a lot of questions."

"Well, I might have some answers," she said, looking up at him with a coquettish smile.

"Really? Should I start asking and we'll see?"

"Well," she said, "you'd have to do somethin' for me, first."

"And what would that be?"

She stepped in close to him, so he could feel the heat from her body.

"What do you think, Mr. Gunsmith?" she asked, putting her hand on his crotch and rubbing.

"So you were listening inside," Clint said. "You know who I am."

"Frank told me."

"Why?"

"He knew I'd be interested."

"And why would you be interested in me?"

"Because you have a reputation."

"What good does my reputation do you?" he asked.

She rubbed him again and said, "That depends on which reputation you think I'm talkin' about."

"Oh."

"See," she said, "there ain't a decent man in this town, and it's been a while since I been . . . satisfied."

"I see."

"So, you satisfy me, and I'll answer your questions."

"And where would you like to do this?" he asked. "Up in your room?"

"I don't have a room here," she said, "and my place is too far from here, so . . ." She backed up, pressed against the wall. ". . . right here will do."

She reached down, raised her dress to her waist, revealing that she was naked underneath. Her thighs were milky white, and the hairy patch between her legs was black as night.

It was also sexy as hell!

Chapter Fourteen

Clint looked around. Was this girl on the level, or was she setting him up for somebody? Get him all involved in pinning her to the wall, and then attack him?

He was wearing a jacket against the Minnesota chill, but it was short, so it wouldn't impede his access to his gun. Now he unbuttoned it.

"What's wrong?" she asked, holding her dress up with one hand, and probing herself with the other. "Too good to be true? Come on, I'm all wet. See?" She showed him her glistening fingertips.

He knew she was wet and ready. He could not only see it but smell it.

"There's nobody here but you and me, Gunsmith," she said. "Come on, give it to me."

So far she was right. There was nobody there but them, so why not?

He moved close enough for her to put those wet fingers behind his neck and pull him close for a kiss. When she broke the kiss, she pressed the wet fingers to his mouth. He put his tongue out and licked them—and he was done.

He unbuttoned his pants, took out his hard dick and maneuvered to slide it right into her—and he was still wearing his gunbelt! Whether it was just going to be them, or somebody was going to come out of the woodwork and attack him, he had them both covered.

"Oh, God, yeah," she said.

He reached down with both hands to cup her butt and lifted her up higher against the wall and started pumping in and out of her. At the first sign of trouble he'd be able to drop her and draw his gun. Neither of them was affected by the cold breeze on their bare, wet skin. Besides, her skin and pussy were hot, heating him up nicely.

He was getting more excited. Anybody could have walked by the mouth of alley, looked in and seen what they were doing.

"Oh, yeah, come on," she said, now wrapping both arms around his neck and bouncing up and down on his cock. "You're givin' it to me!"

"Yeah, I am," he agreed, growling as he tried to give it to her even harder. Once or twice he took her away from the wall, then banged her right up against it again. She didn't complain. Not once.

By now he was positive this was just what it seemed to be, sex in the alley with nobody else around. He no longer feared any kind of attack. Frank the bartender had told her who he was, and she ran out to the alley to ambush him and get him to do this.

He didn't mind.

He stared into her face, which was scrunched up as she bit her lips to keep from screaming. That would have brought people running into that alley, for sure.

She grunted, and growled, and moaned, then leaned forward to bite him to keep from screaming in his ear.

The aroma of her was filling his nostrils and he decided to do something about it. So he set her down on her feet, withdrew from her despite her efforts to keep him inside of her, and went down to his knees. He lifted the dress, got underneath, and buried his face in her wetness. She lifted one leg and draped it over his shoulder to open herself up to him. As he licked and nipped at her she gasped, reached to hold his head in place through the dress, and once again tried to muffle her cries of pleasure.

"Oh Gunsmith," she said, "get it, Gunsmith, lick it, bite me, oh yeah . . ." Anything she said after that was garbled as he worked her into a frenzy, until she gushed all over his face, wetting him thoroughly. He had been with all kinds of women: dry ones, wet ones, those who squirted, those who simply . . . well, seeped. This one was a gusher, but he didn't mind because he loved all women. All sizes, shapes, ages, whether they were dribblers or gushers . . .

When her legs stopped trembling he stood, lifted her and once again jammed his cock into her. This time he slammed her against the wall until he finally exploded inside of her, and they both muffled their cries with kisses . . .

***

"I don't think I can walk yet," she said, straightening her dress.

"Me, neither," he replied, buttoning his trousers. Now he was feeling the cold, and also buttoned his jacket.

"You had that gun on the whole time?" she asked him.

"It didn't get in the way, did it?" he answered.

"I guess not," she said. "I guess when you're with the Gunsmith you have to be aware that you might get shot at."

"That's why I usually try to do what we just did behind closed doors," he said.

"We could try that, next time," she commented.

"By the way," he said, "now you have to fulfill your part of the bargain."

"Oh, that," she said, "well, you can ask me questions, but I don't know how helpful my answers will be."

Clint got the impression he'd been had, but he really couldn't complain about it.

"Have you spent much time with Dutch men since you came to town?" he asked.

"Not really," she said. "The majority of the Bottom's customers are regular Westerners."

"Have you heard any of them talking about Little Amsterdam?"

"In what way?"

"The town just seems very . . . positive," he said. "Almost too good to be true."

"Wow," she said, smoothing her hair, "I've said the same thing myself once or twice, to Frank."

"Are you and Frank . . ."

"What? Together? Oh, no, I just work for him. And we talk."

"About the town?"

"About anything," she said. "Like he told you, today's a busy day for his place. Usually, it's just him and me."

A couple of men walked past and peered into the alley at them.

"Maybe it's time for us to get out of here," he said.

"I have to go back to work," she said, as they did so. He walked her to the batwing doors. "Will you be comin' back?" she asked him.

"Probably," Clint said. "I'm still looking for some answers."

"Why not just leave town?" she asked. "Just keep on movin'?"

"I don't know," he said, "I really don't . . . there's something about this town . . ."

She put her hand on his arm. "Come back and see me."

"Just make sure Frank keeps that glass clean for me," he said.

She laughed and went through the doors.

Chapter Fifteen

When Clint got to his hotel the clerk looked very excited.

"Mr. Adams!" he called.

"What is it?" Clint asked, approaching the desk.

"He was here, looking for you," the clerk said.

"Who was?"

"Gustav. He hardly ever comes to town and he was here, asking for you."

"When?"

"Earlier this afternoon."

"Did he say what he wanted?"

"No," the clerk said, "just that he was looking for you."

"And did he say where he would be?"

"No, sir," the clerk said, "he just left."

Clint turned and went back out. Gustav was probably looking to get that shooting lesson. They hadn't made any arrangements for the lesson to be today.

He stood out in front of the hotel and wondered what Gustav would do, where he'd go? Back to the ranch, or would he stick around and keep looking? He hadn't seen the man in any of the saloons he'd been in.

He decided to go to the Dutchman. That was probably the place Gustav would drink.

As he walked in he saw the saloon was starting to pick up business as it got later in the day. In any other town, the cloths would have been taken off the gaming tables by now, and the girls would be working the floor.

The same bartender, whose name he had never gotten, smiled and beckoned him over to the bar.

"You just missed Gustav," he said. "He was here a few minutes ago."

"He was looking for me at my hotel," Clint said. "I thought I'd check and see if he was here."

"Well, he was," the man said, "but now he's moved on."

"Did he mention me?"

"No, sir. He had a beer, looked around, didn't speak to anyone, and then left."

"Didn't say where he was heading next?"

"Not a word."

"Well, okay," Clint said. "I guess I'll just keep looking for him."

"Come back for a beer later."

"I will." He headed for the door.

"And bring Gustav if you find him," he called out. "Can't be bad for business to have him be seen drinkin' here."

"Gotcha!"

***

When Clint left the Dutchman, he didn't know quite where to go. How would Gustav spend his time in town if he wasn't drinking or taking shooting lessons? What other business might he be taking care of?

When he spotted the office of the High Commissioner across the street, he decided to try that.

Abraham De Jong glared up from his desk. Clint looked around, saw everything he'd see in a sheriff's office—a pot-bellied stove with a coffee pot sitting on it, a rifle rack on the wall, cell keys hanging on a wall peg.

"Mr. Adams," De Jong said. "What can I do for you?"

"Well," Clint said, hunching his shoulders, "it's a little chilly out. A cup of coffee would be good."

"My pleasure." De Jong walked to the stove, picked up the pot and grabbed a mug from nearby. Then he turned to Clint and held the pot aloft.

"I warn you, it's Dutch."

"That's fine."

De Jong handed him a mug, then took one for himself and sat behind his desk.

"Have a seat and tell me what I can do for you," the High Commissioner said.

"Gustav and I are going around town, missing each other," Clint said. "Where can I find him?"

"Who knows?" De Jong said. "He could be buying supplies for his ranch, which means the mercantile, the leather shop, the food and grain, the livery . . ."

"Okay, okay," Clint said, "I get it. You don't know where he is."

"Gustav does not check in with me," De Jong said. "The fact is, he doesn't talk to me very much, at all."

"And why's that?"

"He appointed me High Commissioner," De Jong said, "but we've never liked each other, very much."

"Were you acquainted before he built this town?" Clint asked.

"We were, in New York. I came because he said he needed law and order here."

"So even though he doesn't like you, and you don't like him . . ."

"We respect each other."

"That's . . . nice."

"It's a nice town," De Jong said, sitting back.

Clint looked at the keys on the wall peg.

"Does that mean you never use your cells?"

"Oh, on occasion somebody will get too drunk and need to sleep it off," De Jong said, "but that's about all. We've been here over a year and have had no gun play and no bank robberies."

"Over a year," Clint repeated.

"Well," De Jong said, "that's how long I've been here. Before that some of the buildings were up, but it's only been about a year since the town was christened Little Amsterdam."

Clint sipped the coffee, enjoying the heat if nothing else.

"Have you walked the entire town?" De Jong asked.

"Pretty much."

"And what do you think?"

"Like you say," Clint replied, "a nice, quiet town."

"Someplace you'd like to settle?"

"I'm not Dutch."

"That doesn't matter," De Jong said, "we have people here who are not Dutch."

"I'm not the settling type," Clint added.

"Well, if you change your mind," De Jong said, "we're here."

Clint finished his coffee, stood, set the cup down on De Jong's desk and said, "I'll sure keep that in mind."

Chapter Sixteen

Clint left the High Commissioner's office more convinced than ever that something was bubbling beneath the surface of Little Amsterdam. The only problem was, nobody would talk about it. He needed to find somebody—somebody Dutch—who wasn't toeing the mark.

He wondered if that would be a man, or a woman?

Across the street he saw somebody familiar walking quickly, realized it was the girl, the waitress, he'd seen on his first day. She was hurrying, and he wondered if she was going to work at her father's café, or home from the café.

He followed, keeping to his side of the street.

She moved quickly, ducking around slower moving people as she went. They didn't even turn to look at her. Then she went down a side street, so he hurried across so he could stay with her.

Other bystanders nodded at him as he went by, just as a greeting. They nodded and waved as she went past.

This was not the direction of the café. Possibly, he was following her home.

He found himself in a part of town he had not walked yet. The further they went, the less people there were on the street. Finally they reached an area that looked as if it was just homes, no businesses.

The houses all looked new, one and two story structures mixed in with each other. The blonde girl went to a one story house, scurried up the walk and let herself in with a key.

So she was going home, and in a hurry.

Clint looked around. There was no movement in any of the other houses. But he didn't want anyone to see him standing there.

Now he knew where the girl lived and worked, and she was the first thing that had interested him about the town.

No, she was the second.

The town itself was the first, and it still was.

He turned and headed back to the business part of town.

***

He felt foolish, following the girl home. Where did he think she was going to lead him. To the answers to his questions?

He got back to Little Amsterdam's main street, but didn't feel comfortable there. Funny, but the only place he'd felt comfortable since arriving was the little dirty saloon, The Bottom. Instead of continuing to look for Gustav, he went there.

Chapter Seventeen

"Back so soon?' Frank asked, as Clint entered.

"I've been thinking about that clean glass."

"Comin' up," Frank said, with a grin.

It looked as if the same customers were still there, but Miley wasn't around.

"Here ya go." Frank set the mug of beer in front of him. "You find out anythin'?"

"Not really," Clint said. "I did find a part of town I hadn't seen before. All houses."

"Ah," Frank said, "the posh part of town. That's where the people with the money live."

"Where do you live?" Clint asked, after a sip.

"Upstairs. It ain't much, but it's mine."

"What about Miley?"

"Upstairs? Naw, she's got her own room, not far from here," Frank told him. "In fact, she's there now. Said she had to . . . freshen up."

Clint ignored the comment, and the pointed look that followed it.

"This is the only place in town where I feel comfortable," he said.

"That's how these fellas feel," Kelton said, gesturing with one arm to the few customers he had. "That's why they're here, drinkin'. If I could I'd have some tables for them to gamble on."

"So what would happen if you put a faro table, say . . . there?" he asked, pointing.

"I suppose that High Commissioner De Jong would shut me down," Kelton said. "Why, would you want to deal faro in here?"

Clint thought about his friends, Wyatt Earp and Luke Short, both of whom had dealt faro in various saloons over the years.

"No, that's not why I was asking."

"But—hell, that would bring some folks in here. Maybe even some Dutchies, to see the Gunsmith dealin' faro."

"I'm not ready to start breaking the law here in Little Amsterdam," Clint said.

"What do you wanna do, then?"

"I'm not even sure," Clint said. "I just came here to have a look, now I'm trying to find out what's going on beneath the surface. And why?"

"Because you're curious."

"Right, my curiosity. That's what's probably going to get me killed, one day."

"That or some backshooter."

"And that."

Clint turned and looked at the corner he'd pointed out to Kelton. A faro table would fit there very nicely.

"Why do they allow drinking and whores," he asked, turning to face Kelton, "and not gambling?"

"I don't know," the bartender said, shrugging. "I'm not even sure they allow whores."

"What about Miley?"

"She's a saloon girl, not a whore."

"But earlier you asked me if I was interested in spending time with her."

"Yeah," Kelton said, "talkin'."

"Oh."

"Have you seen any whores in town, at the other saloon?"

"Now that you mention it," Clint said, "no. I just thought Miley—"

"Again," Kelton said, "she's not a whore."

"Right." At that moment Clint could not recall having seen a saloon girl in any of the other saloons. "Okay, so they allow drinking, but no gambling, and probably no prostitutes."

Kelton was staring at the corner, as well.

"You know, the more I think about it, the more I like the idea," he said. "And we're different from the other saloons in town. A faro table would make us even more different."

"It's a thought," Clint said, "but you'd have to send away for a table, get a dealer—"

"Still thinkin' about you."

"—and then see how the town reacted, once the word got out."

"That the Gunsmith was dealin' faro." Kelton wasn't quite ready to give up on this new dream.

"But what if this town is just what it appears to be?" Clint asked.

"Which is?" Kelton asked.

"A nice place to live."

"You mean, a boring place to live," Kelton said. "Besides, now you sound just like the rest of 'em. 'A happy and pleasant place to live.' I'm so tired of hearin' that."

"It's as if they've all been coached on what to say."

"That's right."

"Gustav!" Clint said.

"What?"

"Gustav," Clint said, again, "he's the one I have to talk to. He founded the town. He also made all the rules, right?"

"Right."

"And De Jong just enforces them."

"Right, again," Kelton said. "So how are you gonna get close to Gustav?"

"I already am," Clint said. "He's been looking for me all afternoon."

"For what?"

"He asked me to teach him how to shoot."

"What're you gonna do?"

"I'm going to teach him," Clint said, "and while I'm doing that I'll try and get a look beneath the surface."

"Of Gustav?"

"Of the town," Clint said. "Of that phrase, 'happy and pleasant.'"

"Well, while you're at it," Kelton said, "see if you can get him to lift the ban on gamblin'."

"I'll bring it up and see what he says."

Clint turned to leave.

"And think again about dealin' faro in here," Kelton said. "After all, it was your idea."

"I didn't mean that I—" Clint started, but he stopped short. "Okay, maybe I'll even approach Gustav about that and see how he reacts."

As he went out the batwing doors Kelton shouted out, "And let me know how it goes!"

Clint waved without turning.

Chapter Eighteen

If Gustav was still in town this long he'd probably be look-ing for someplace to eat supper. Unless he simply went back home to his ranch.

Of course, it wasn't important that Clint found the man that day. Tomorrow would do just as well, and it would be earlier. He decided to go and talk to De Jong about subjects of gam-bling and prostitution.

When he got across the street from the Commissioner's office, the door opened and a man stepped out. It took Clint a moment, but he recognized him as the foreman of the Vanderhoff ranch, Rance Edwards.

Edwards was not Dutch. Maybe he was somebody Clint should talk to, find out why the man took the job working on a ranch owned by a Dutchman, near a town full of Dutch.

As he watched the man started walking. He decided to fol-low him, put off talking to De Jong for later.

He figured Edwards was either going to a saloon for a drink, looking for Gustav, or getting to his horse to return home.

He was wrong on all counts.

***

It took a few minutes, but Clint finally realized where Rance Edwards was going. As he continued to follow, the man took the same route the blonde girl, Gerta, had taken earlier. He led Clint to the neighborhood of homes where bartender Frank Kelton said those with money lived. It didn't take long to discover which house he was going to.

Edwards went up the walk of the same house Gerta had gone into and knocked at the door. When she opened it, she threw her arms around the foreman, and they shared a passionate kiss before Edwards pushed her inside, looked around to see if anyone had spotted them.

Very interesting. But all it meant was that Edwards and Gerta were having a romance, possibly in secret. Given the way the girl's father had watched Clint when he ate at their café, he was sure it was a secret. Clint wondered who actually lived in the house they were using?

He thought about crossing over and peering in the windows but knew what he'd find them doing. And this wasn't part of his curiosity about the town, so he decided to let the two have their privacy. He made his way back to the center of town, and approached the High Commissioner's office, again.

He tried the door and found it locked. There was no reply to his knock. Clint had never seen any indication that the Commissioner had a deputy. De Jong had either gone off duty or went to find some supper.

Thinking about who was going to supper, and what the waitress, Gerta, was doing had made Clint hungry. He went to see if he could find Gustav or De Jong in the vicinity of a steak?

Clint looked in one or two restaurants without finding either Gustav or the High Commissioner, but then decided to go to the small café he'd first seen Gerta and her father in. That was where he finally found De Jong, seated at a table in the front window.

De Jong saw him through the window and nodded to him, and Clint entered.

"Were you looking for me, Mr. Adams?" the High Commissioner asked.

"I was."

"Well, why don't you join me?"

Clint noticed that while De Jong's seat afforded him a view out the window, the seat right across from him sat against a blank wall between the window and the front door. It would put his back to the door but would not make him visible from the outside.

He sat across from De Jong, but instead of facing the man, he moved the chair so that his back was to the wall. That way he could see the room, and the front door.

"You're a very cautious man," De Jong commented.

"It's how I've stayed alive this long."

De Jong cut into the piece of meat he had in front of him. It was a steak but prepared in some Dutch manner.

"I suppose you think I'm foolish to be sitting in front of this window," he said, "but I like to keep an eye on the town even during supper."

"That's up to you," Clint said.

"We don't have gunmen in Little Amsterdam, Mr. Adams," De Jong said. "At least, we didn't until you arrived."

"Are you telling me to leave?"

"Not at all," De Jong said. "Apparently, Gustav likes having you here."

"Is he still in town?"

"I believe he went back to the ranch, but he will be returning tomorrow for his shooting lessons," De Jong said.

"Well," Clint said, "as long as I know that, I'll make myself available."

"What's on your mind that brought you here looking for me?" De Jong asked.

"I really don't want to interrupt your supper," Clint said. "Why don't I come by your office a little later and we can talk. I just have a few questions."

Clint noticed that in the absence of his daughter, her father was waiting tables himself. Every time he passed Clint and De Jong, he gave Clint a hard look.

"Would you care to join me for supper?" the Commissioner asked.

"No, thanks," Clint said. "I don't think Gerta's father wants me here." He stood up. "I'll see you later."

"I look forward to it," De Jong said.

Chapter Nineteen

Clint decided to eat in his hotel's dining room, and simply have a steak to no Dutch trimmings. The room was crowded with diners, but he was still able to secure a back table, away from the door.

After he ordered he looked around, and all he saw were smiling faces—men, women, and children. They all seemed to be very happy with their lot in life. They were apparently very pleased to be living in Little Amsterdam—probably because it was a 'happy and pleasant' place to live and raise children.

As the waiter refilled his coffee cup he asked the young man, "Are you happy?"

"Sir?"

"With your job, and where you live? Are you happy?"

"Well, yes, sir, I suppose so," the man said. "I mean, I don't want to be a waiter forever, but I like living here."

"Why?"

"Well . . . it's happy and pleasant."

"Thanks," Clint said, "for the coffee."

"Yes, sir."

***

When he finished eating he went out to the lobby, which unlike the dining room wasn't crowded. In fact, at the moment there was nobody there but the young desk clerk.

"You mind if I ask you a question?" Clint approached the front desk.

"Well, all right, Mr. Adams."

"Are you happy?"

"I don't—what?"

"Happy," Clint said. "Are you happy here in Little Amsterdam?"

"Well . . . yes," the young man said. "I mean, I don't want to be a desk clerk my whole life, but I like where I live. It's happy and pleasant, here."

"Yeah, I figured you'd say that."

Clint turned just as a man came down the stairs. Their eyes met briefly, and then the man walked through the lobby and out the door.

"Who was that fellow?" Clint asked.

"Who, that? Uh, that was Mr. DeVries."

"DeVries?"

"Yessir."

Clint looked at the door the man had gone through.

"Looked like somebody I should know," he said. "How long's he been here?"

"Long time, sir," the clerk said. "He lives in the hotel."

"What's he do?"

"Do?"

"Yes," Clint said, looking at the clerk, who seemed to be getting nervous, "does he own a business?"

"I ain't exactly sure what he does, sir," the clerk said. "We've got lots of guests. I don't know what they do."

"Huh."

"Anything else, sir?"

"No," Clint said, "not a thing."

Now he had something else to ask High Commissioner De Jong about.

***

Clint went to his room, read for an hour, then left to go to De Jong's office.

"Come on in," De Jong said as Clint opened the door. "I've been expecting you. Coffee?"

"Sure."

"Have a seat."

"I'll stand," Clint said. "I've been sitting."

"Suit yourself," De Jong said, sitting. "What's on your mind now?"

"I've been wondering about the rules in this town."

"Which rules are those?"

"First, no gambling. What's the point of that?"

"Saves having to clean up after a couple of gamblers get mad about losing and try to kill each other."

"And whores?"

"What about them?"

"I don't see any in the saloons."

"We've got them," De Jong said. "We know that men sometimes need a release."

"So where are they?"

"In one building."

"Is the no gambling a rule, or the law?" Clint asked.

"Well now," De Jong said, "it's sort of a rule that's enforced like a law."

"So let's say somebody—like me, for instance—decides to deal some faro in one of the saloons. Would you shut me down?"

"If Gustav tells me to, I will."

"So you'd have to check with him first."

De Jong nodded. "He made the rules."

"What if I'm dealing in a saloon not frequented by Dutch people?"

"I don't know if that matters, Mr. Adams," De Jong said. "I know of only one such saloon. The Bottom. Is that what you're talking about?"

"Yes, it is."

"Well," De Jong said, "we'd just as soon that place close its doors."

"Have you told the owner that?"

"Not in so many words, no."

"Well, maybe you should, so it's clear to the owner, Frank Kelton."

"I know Kelton," De Jong said, but didn't go any further.

Clint started for the door, stopping before he got there.

"One other thing."

"Yes?"

"There's a man staying at the same hotel I am, his name is DeVries. Do you know him?"

"I believe I know the man you're speaking of."

"Do you know what he does?"

"I think Mr. DeVries is a recent arrival," De Jong said, "and that he's still trying to decide what he will do here."

"You don't know what he did before he came here?" Clint asked.

"That really doesn't matter, Mr. Adams," De Jong said. "If anyone decides they want to settle here—man, woman or family—it only matters what they will do to be a productive part of the community."

"Uh-huh," Clint said.

"Why? Do you know Mr. DeVries?"

"He looked familiar, is all," Clint said. "Thanks for your time, Commissioner."

"Stop in whenever you want, Mr. Adams," De Jong said. "I'm always glad to help."

Clint nodded, and left the man's office.

Chapter Twenty

Clint left the office not liking the way he was feeling.

More and more he became convinced that he'd seen that fellow in the hotel before, and his name wasn't DeVries. It was going to come to him, and when it did he thought it might explain a lot.

He was trying to decide between going to his hotel or to the Bottom Saloon when he saw Rance Edwards, the foreman from the Vanderhoff ranch. He was coming down the street, possibly heading for the livery stable. He crossed to intersect with him.

"Mr. Edwards," he said.

The man saw him and came to a stop.

"Mr. Adams. Somethin' I can do for you?"

"Did you happen to ride in with Gustav today?" Clint asked him.

"No, I didn't, I had some other business to take care of. But I know he rode in to look for you," Edwards said. "He wants those shootin' lessons."

"You're not Dutch, Mr. Edwards," Clint said. "You're a Westerner. Why don't you teach him how to shoot?"

"I could do that," Edwards said, "but I know horses better than I know guns, Mr. Adams. I could never teach him to shoot the way you could."

"Well, I'm sorry we kept missing each other today," Clint said. "Would you tell him that I'll make myself available to him tomorrow, if he'll come by my hotel?"

"I'm on my way back to the ranch right now," Edwards said. "I'll tell him."

"Thank you."

Edwards started for the livery again, and Clint couldn't help himself.

"Mr. Edwards."

The foreman turned. "If you're gonna be around here some longer, Adams, you better call me Rance."

"And you can call me Clint. You mind me asking what business brought you to town today?"

"Oh," Edwards said, "that was somethin' that was, uh, real personal."

"It was, huh?"

"Yessir."

Clint was going to mention seeing him with the girl but changed his mind.

"Well," Clint said, "I appreciate you delivering my message."

"No problem," Edwards said and continued to the livery.

Chapter Twenty-One

Clint spent most of the evening in the Bottom, talking with Frank Kelton and exchanging looks with Miley. She didn't seem to want Kelton to know about their alley rendezvous—even though it had been the bartender who told her Clint was the Gunsmith.

"So who do you think this fella is you saw at the hotel?" Kelton asked.

"It's nagging at me," Clint said, "but I know his name's not DeVries, and he's not Dutch."

Kelton rubbed his jaw, thoughtfully.

"So how many others do you think are in town pretendin' to be Dutch?"

"I don't know, but why would they be doing that?"

"To fit in?" the bartender suggested.

"But fit in where? How? As a Dutch cabinet maker? Or baker?"

"Or bartender?" Kelton offered.

"Right."

Something occurred to Clint at that moment.

"Frank, what did you have to do to open this place?" he asked.

"I hadda get liquor, hire Miley, get these tables and chairs—"

"I mean, did you have to pay anything? To the town?"

"Oh, yeah," he said. "They called it a start-up fee."

"And did everybody who wanted to open a business in Little Amsterdam have to pay?"

"I don't know," Kelton said. "I guess so."

"Frank . . . do you have a record? Are you wanted anywhere?"

"What? Me, no!"

"Did they give you a hard time when you came here?"

"Well, yeah, how do you think I ended up with this dump. They didn't wanna give me anything on the main streets."

"Did you ever think about leaving?"

"Well, yeah, but then I thought, fuck it. I ain't lettin' them chase me outta town."

Clint nodded, sipped his beer.

"What are you gettin' at?"

"Well, the only time I've been in a place like this before," Clint said, "was when it was, you know, an outlaw town. Like a safe place for outlaws to live, that other folks didn't know about. And if somebody wandered in by accident, they'd just think it was a normal town."

"So you think that's what Little Amsterdam is? An outlaw town?"

"I'm just sayin''

"And Gustav is . . . what? The gang leader?"

Clint shrugged.

"So you think I wandered in, they couldn't get rid of me, so they gave me this dump?"

"Better than killing you."

"And what about Miley? Is she an outlaw?"

"Where'd you find her?"

Kelton scratched his beard stubble.

"On the road," he said. "She was just ridin', and I offered her a job . . . if I got a place."

"So she rode in with you?"

"Yeah."

"Did you make out like you were a couple?"

"Well, just for a while," Kelton said, "so nobody would bother her. There weren't never anythin' between us."

"And what about these fellas?" Clint asked, indicating Kelton's clientele.

"They're like you," Kelton said. "They rode in, didn't feel comfortable, so they spend most of their days here. If this is an outlaw hideout, then why are they lettin' us stay here?"

"I don't know," Clint said. "But the more I think about it, the more sense it makes. Because all that happy and pleasant stuff? That doesn't make sense to me."

"Never made sense to me, neither," Kelton admitted.

"And that man, DeVries . . . I need to get a better look at him," Clint said. "Once I remember who he is, I may have the answers."

"What're you gonna do?"

"Is there a telegraph office here?"

"No," Kelton said. "There's no telegraph office, no stage office, no church."

"See?" Clint said. "No stage. That's another indication."

"So what're you gonna do?" Kelton asked again.

"Tomorrow I start Gustav's shooting lessons," Clint said. "And maybe I'll get a better look at DeVries. Hopefully, by tomorrow night, I'll either know more, or be sure of more."

"And you'll let us know?"

Clint finished his beer.

"I'll let you know," Clint said. "Meanwhile, you might as well just keep doing what you're doing."

"Which is nothin'," Kelton said.

"Right," Clint said, "the safest thing for you and Miley and the others here right now is to do nothing."

Chapter Twenty-Two

When Rance Edwards got back to the ranch he found Gustav on the porch, drinking brandy, smoking a cigar, surveying what he owned.

"Do you want some?" he asked, raising the glass to Edwards as he came up onto the porch.

"No, thanks."

"Are you just back from town?"

"Yes. I saw Clint Adams."

"Oh, I was looking for him today," Gustav said. "What did he say?"

"That he'll be ready for you tomorrow," Edwards said. "Your lessons can begin."

"Is that all?"

"He asked me why I didn't teach you to shoot."

"And what did you tell him?"

"That I couldn't do it the way he could," the foreman said.

"That's good," Gustav said. "And did he ask any other questions?"

Edwards thought about Gerta, the waitress, and said, "No."

"That is good."

Edwards stood there for a few more moments, and then Gustav looked at him, rolling the cigar between his lips.

"Is there something else?"

"Is everything goin' okay?"

"Everything is fine, Rance," Gustav said.

"Do you think Adams is gonna stay?"

"I don't know," Gustav said. "Who knows how much of the man is fact and how much is fiction? Maybe I can find out, starting tomorrow."

"Why would we need him?"

"What do you think of De Jong? As High Commissioner."

"I think it's silly," Edwards said. "He should just be sheriff."

"But what do you think of him as the rule keeper?"

Edwards shrugged.

"Doesn't seem to me he's had to do much," he said. "Nobody's breakin' the rules."

"Yet," Gustav said. "What happens when somebody does?"

"Why would they?" Edwards asked. "Everybody's happy here."

"Yes," Gustav said, "everybody."

"Is there a problem I need to know about?" the foreman asked.

"No, Rance," Gustav said, "you know all you need to know. Good-night."

"Good-night, Gustav."

Edwards went back down the stairs and headed for the bunkhouse.

***

In the barn, where everybody knew better than to enter when the doors were closed, Abraham De Jong rolled off of

Hilda Vanderhoff and laid beside her on the hay bed they had just used.

"Catch your breath," she told him, "and then you have to leave."

"Sure."

She sat up, her large, pendulous breasts swaying with the movement. He reached out and took one in his hand.

"Why don't we leave here?" he asked.

"Together?"

"Sure, why not?" he said. "What do you have with Gustav?"

"Money, a ranch, and a town. What would I have with you, Abraham."

He grabbed her hand and put it on his semi-hard cock.

"This."

When he released her, she patted his cock and then pulled her hand away.

"There are a lot of these here," she said. "I can get one whenever I want. The fact that you are here with me proves that."

"How long do you think Gustav is going to let you keep doing this?" he asked.

"As long as I can do it," she said, "or until he dies. One of the two."

"And what if he kills you?" he asked. "Or has somebody else do it?"

"No one would dare," she said. "Besides, he would not kill me. He loves me."

"You think so?" he asked. "After all the times you've humiliated him?"

She stood up, began to pull on her dress. When her luscious, naked body was covered up, De Jong felt a sense of loss.

"I have never humiliated him," she said. "For that he would have to be unaware of what goes on."

"So he knows you do this?"

"Of course he does," she said. "I would not lie to my husband."

"You two have the oddest relationship," he said. "I don't understand it."

"You don't have to," she said. "All you have to do is come when I call."

He was getting dressed as she went out the front doors.

***

Gustav was reading when she reentered the house. She didn't bother him, and went right up to her bedroom, which was separate from his.

She grabbed her nightgown, went down the hall to the indoor water closet Gustav had built into the house. She filled the bathtub, got in and soaked in the hot water, thinking that she needed a change from these men in Little Amsterdam. She needed somebody better, somebody different.

While she was drying herself, she thought that the only different man in town was the Gunsmith. She could tell that just from the little time she spent with him at supper, with

Gustav. He wasn't afraid of Gustav, but then he didn't know who her husband really was.

She put on her nightgown and walked to her bedroom. Tomorrow she would go into town and find Clint Adams. It shouldn't be that hard to get what she wanted from him. He was, after all, a man.

And she knew how to get what she wanted from a man. She had been doing it her whole life.

Chapter Twenty-Three

The next morning Clint had breakfast and then sat out in front of the hotel. He watched the town go by, hoping that the man DeVries would come down eventually. He just needed another look at him. And if Gustav happened by early, that would work, too.

If he was right and this town was an outlaw hideout it was unlike any other he'd ever seen. Maybe Gustav had these people convinced to put their past behind them and start over in a "happy and pleasant" town. That was why they'd allowed Frank Kelton to open a place and cater to people who weren't "Dutch." He wondered how many actual Dutch folks there were in Little Amsterdam? Gustav certainly seemed to be, along with his wife and his cook, but who else? De Jong? Possibly. Maybe the Dutch part of the town was on the level. After all, he'd had some Dutch food and beer. Some of the other people looked and sounded Dutch.

But not DeVries. He was pretty damn sure of that.

A few people left the hotel, but DeVries was not among them.

Finally, a man stepped through the front door of the hotel and stopped to light a cigarette. He was standing about 10 feet away from Clint, but in that moment, it didn't matter if it was 50 feet.

Clint knew him.

Or rather he knew who he was.

The man turned his head, saw Clint, then turned and quickly walked the other way.

***

"He's who?" Frank Kelton asked.

It was early, and the Bottom really wasn't open yet. Clint had banged on the door until Kelton answered it, let him in, and gave him a cup of coffee. He also apologized but said he really didn't have anyone to talk to about this.

"His name is Darius Collier," Clint said. "He rode with the Youngers and James boys, years ago, but not on the Northfield Raid." The Northfield Raid was the last job the Youngers ever pulled.

"So what's he doin' here now if he wasn't in Minnesota back then?"

"Hiding where he figures nobody would look for him," Clint said.

"What's he been doin' since he left the James/Younger Gang?" Kelton asked.

"Probably pulling his own jobs."

"Does he know you recognized him?"

"I think so."

"Will he try to kill you?"

"Maybe," Clint said. "I don't know if he's got anybody here watching his back."

"And you've got nobody watchin' yours."

"That's true."

"I'd offer to help," Kelton said, "but I'm a bartender, not a gunman."

"You are helping, Frank," Clint said. "Just by letting me come here and talk this out with you."

"I wish I could do more."

Clint stood up. "Thanks for the coffee."

"What are you gonna do?" Kelton said, walking him to the door.

"I'm not sure, but I think I'm going to talk to Collier, see if I can't find out from him what the hell's going on here."

"And if he won't tell you?"

"Then I'll ask him again," Clint said, "only this time harder."

Chapter Twenty-Four

He returned to the hotel, where he had left a message with the desk clerk for Gustav, if he showed up.

"No, sir," the clerk sad, "Gustav hasn't been in since you left."

"Okay, thanks."

"Would you like to leave another message?"

"No," Clint said, "I'll just sit outside and wait for him."

Clint left the lobby and took up his position in front of the hotel again.

***

Frank Kelton looked up from the bar when he heard the front door open, was surprised to see High Commissioner De Jong enter his place.

"Well," he said, "Commissioner, what can I do for you?"

De Jong looked around, distaste plain on his face.

"I understand the Gunsmith has been frequenting your place," De Jong said.

"Uh, yeah, that's right," Kelton said. "I guess he feels more comfortable here than in some of the other places in town."

Miley was at her position at the end of the bar, listening intently.

"That so?"

"You'd have to ask him," Kelton said, "but that's why these varmints are here."

De Jong glanced around at the three customers in the place, two at tables and one at the bar. None of them looked back at him. Then he looked at the girl, who stared back at him, boldly.

"I would think he'd have better taste than this," he said.

"Somethin' else I can do for you?" Kelton asked.

"What's he talk about when he's here?" De Jong asked. "Adams."

"The weather."

De Jong narrowed his eyes at Kelton, who didn't back down.

"You know I could close you down if I wanted to," he said.

"And why would you do that?"

"Because you're uncooperative."

"And here I thought I was answerin' all your question," Kelton said. He looked at Miley. "Ain't I answerin' all his questions?"

"That's what it sounds like to me," she said.

"Are you a whore, young lady?" De Jong asked. "Seems to me Adams was looking for some whores. Is that what he found here?"

"Clint Adams don't pay for whores," she said.

"You know him that well, then?"

"We just met him," Kelton said, "but yeah, we think we know him pretty well."

De Jong looked back at the bartender.

"Are your fees up to date?" he asked.

"Guess you'll have to check," Kelton said.

"I will," De Jong said, "and then I'll be back."

"I'll have a glass waitin' for you," Kelton said, and thought, the dirtiest one I got.

"Don't bother," De Jong said. "I wouldn't drink here if you paid me."

With that he left, and Miley came down the bar to Kelton.

"Maybe Clint should know that he was here askin' about him," she suggested.

"That sounds like a good idea," Kelton said. "Why don't you go find 'im and tell 'im?"

"I'll be back," she said.

She got a shawl from the back room and headed for Clint's hotel.

***

When De Jong got back to his office he found Gustav there, waiting for him.

"Why do we let that Bottom Saloon operate?" he asked.

"We just needed something different," Gustav said. "We don't want folks comin' here and thinkin' they can't fit in."

"Well, maybe Adams fits in there a little too well," De Jong said. "I don't like that Kelton. Is he paid up?"

"He is."

"I thought we didn't want folks comin here, at all?" De Jong said, sitting down.

"You see Clint today?"

"I saw him sitting out in front of his hotel," De Jong said. "I think he's waiting for you."

"Where are the men?" Gustav asked.

"Around."

"Why don't you have them pay the Bottom a visit," Gustav said. "I'll keep Adams occupied."

"Why don't we get rid of him?" De Jong asked.

"We just might," Gustav said, "but when I say so."

"Sure."

Gustav left. De Jong thought the man was playing with fire, letting the Gunsmith stay around. Maybe he'd end up getting burnt, and then De Jong could take over.

Maybe that's why Clint Adams was in town. To make that happen. Then Hilda would look at him differently, if he was in charge.

He left the office to find the men and send them to the Bottom Saloon.

Chapter Twenty-Five

Clint saw Miley rushing up the street toward him and stood up to meet her.

"Is something wrong?" he asked.

She took a moment to catch her breath, and he took hold of her arms to steady her.

"De Jong came back to the Bottom," she said. "He was askin' all kinds of questions about you."

"Did Frank answer him, or give him a hard time?" Clint asked.

"A little of both," she said.

"He shouldn't have done that," Clint said. "I don't want him getting into trouble."

"Well, we just thought you outta know about it."

"I appreciate that," Clint said. "What kind of questions was he asking?"

"Wanted to know what you talked about when you came by. Frank told him the weather."

Clint laughed.

"I'll bet that went over big with De Jong. Okay, go back and tell Frank if De Jong comes back he should just answer him. Don't give him a hard time on my account."

"All right, I'll tell him," she said. "I don't like that man much. He called me a whore. I ain't a whore."

"I know that," Clint said, "but don't give him a hard time. I don't want either of you getting into trouble. Okay?"

"Okay," she said. "I'll tell Frank. But you be careful."

"I'm always careful," he said. "Now you get going."

He released her arms. She put her hand on his chest. For a moment he thought she was going to kiss him, but then she turned and ran back the way she came.

***

About half an hour later Clint saw Gustav approaching, crossing the street from the other side. He hadn't seen where the man was coming from.

"Good afternoon," Gustav greeted.

"'afternoon."

Gustav mounted the boardwalk.

"I'm sorry, I meant to be here earlier."

"I'm sorry we kept missing each other yesterday," Clint said, letting the front legs of his chair come down. "You ready?"

"As I'll ever be." He indicated the pistol he had in his belt.

"Let me see that."

Gustav took it out and passed it over.

"Navy Colt," Clint said. "Forty-four. These came out in eighteen-fifty-one, but they're still reliable. Slow, but reliable."

"Well, I am not looking to be a fast gun," Gustav said. "I would just like to hit what I aim at."

"That's your first mistake," Clint said.

"What is that?"

"Aiming."

Gustav looked surprised.

"You do not aim?"

"I don't," Clint said. "I just point and shoot. See, the gun is like my finger. I hit what I point at."

"Amazing. Will I be able to do that?"

"I don't know." Clint passed the gun back. "Let's see."

"Right here?"

There were people on the street, so Clint said, "No, we better find an alley, or an empty lot."

"I know just the place," Gustav said. "Come."

***

Gustav walked him about three blocks to a corner that was a big vacant lot.

"What was here?" Clint asked.

"Nothing," Gustav said. "But we're thinking about building a church here."

"What religion are the Dutch?" Clint asked.

"Mostly Catholic," Gustav replied, "but there are some Protestant."

"What will you build, then?"

"That is what is being discussed."

Clint looked around the lot. There was nothing there to shoot at, except for a few tin cans.

"This'll have to do," Clint said. "Let me see you hit one of those cans."

Gustav took the gun out of his belt.

"Which one?"

"Pick one," Clint said.

The man looked at the three or four tin cans that were lying on the ground. Then he raised the Navy Colt, cocked the hammer, and fired.

He didn't hit a thing but dirt.

"We're going to have a lot of work to do," Clint said, shaking his head.

Chapter Twenty-Six

It didn't take long for Clint to discover that Gustav was hopeless with a gun.

"Why do you think I asked you for lessons?" Gustav asked, laughing.

"Well," Clint said, "it's going to take us more than one day."

"Why don't you come out to the ranch tomorrow and stay for supper?" Gustav asked. "We can practice in the afternoon."

"You don't have any more time today?"

"There's a town not far from here called Riverton," the man said. "I have some business there. We don't have a telegraph office here so I must ride out."

"I see," Clint said. "Well, okay then. I'll come by tomorrow." He wanted to know how far Riverton really was but didn't want to ask Gustav. He'd ask Frank Kelton, later.

They shook hands and went their separate ways, Gustav to the livery stable for his horse, and Clint back to his hotel.

***

When he got to the hotel lobby he thought he probably should have gone to the Bottom Saloon to see Frank Kelton and Miley. After all, they were worried about him, and he had a question for Kelton. But he could see from the desk clerk's nervous demeanor that he had something on his mind.

"What's going on?" he asked the young man.

"Uh, she said it'd be all right, Mr. Adams."

"What would?"

"For me to let her into your room."

"Oh? How long has she been up there?"

"About an hour."

"Okay," Clint said, "thanks."

He went up to the second floor and walked to his door. When he got there, he put his ear to it. Just because the clerk had given his key to a woman didn't mean there was a woman in the room.

He couldn't hear anything, so whoever was in there was being very quiet. He assumed it was Miley. If it was a man—or more than one man, they were really good at keeping quiet and still.

Clint put his right hand on his gun, and his left on the doorknob.

***

When Gustav got to the stable he told the liveryman to saddle his horse.

"Headin' home, Mr. Vanderhoff?" the man asked, saddling it quickly.

"That's what I'm doing, Hans," Gustav said, mounting up. "I'm heading home."

He rode out of town and when he came to the road leading to Riverton he went the other way, toward his ranch.

Clint opened the door quickly and darted into the room, hand ready to draw. But it wasn't necessary.

"Well," Hildegard Vanderhoff said from the bed, "I was wondering if you were ever going to come back to your room."

Clint relaxed his gunhand, closed the door behind him with his left.

"I'm sorry," he said, "I was busy trying to teach your husband to shoot."

"Oh," she said, "he is as useless with a gun as he is with other things."

She was sitting very relaxed, her hands behind her, one leg crossed over the other, clad in a simple cotton dress that was only sexy because of the body underneath it. She had kicked off her shoes; her bare feet were pale and smooth, not as large as one might have expected. It was a foot that made a man think of sex.

He figured she might weigh two hundred pounds, but she was built to be in bed with a man, all curves.

The room was warm, with most of the heat coming off her body.

"Well," she said, "first you must call me Hilda. If we are going to do what we are going to do, we should be on a first name basis."

"And what are we going to do, Hilda?"

She smiled. She was a handsome woman, not a pretty one, but the smile lit up her face and changed that.

"What you knew we were going to do the moment we saw each other, Clint."

Clint didn't pretend not to know what she was referring to.

"How would your husband feel about this?"

"Don't worry about him. It's something he and I have not done for years. As you could probably tell from looking at us, he is quite a bit older than I am."

"Why did you marry him then?"

"First, he had a lot of money and would take care of me. And he has."

"And second?"

"He told me he would take me to see the West." She spread her arms, which made her breasts lift very nicely. "And here we are."

"Well," Clint said, "Minnesota isn't really the West, you know."

"Yes, but we are closer than we were in Philadelphia."

He didn't bother telling her that he had been under the impression they had come from the Netherlands. He thought perhaps this slip of the tongue might come in handy later.

"And what makes you think I'll do it?" he asked.

"You're a man," she said. "Here, let me give you a sample." She stood up, reached behind her and shrugged the dress off. It fell to the floor and she kicked it away. She knew what she had come there for, so she hadn't bothered with any underwear.

He was looking at an embarrassment of riches, bounty beyond belief, large breasts with light nipples and heavy undersides, wide hips, ample thighs and powerful calves. She did a turn one time for him so he could see her wide, inviting ass.

"Well?" she asked.

Clint was breathless, but even so, he had to admit that he had felt more excitement in the alley with Miley. But this . . . this was awe. And the fact that she knew the effect she had on men made it even more powerful.

"I've heard," he said, "that you're pretty active in town."

"And at the ranch," she admitted, "but never with a man like you. And I have heard that you're very active with women."

Touché, he thought. He liked that she didn't back down or try to make excuses.

"All right, then," he said, undoing his gunbelt.

Chapter Twenty-Seven

But he wasn't about to get careless.

There was still the possibility she was setting him up, so he took precautions. He grabbed the wooden chair in the room and jammed it underneath the doorknob. Then he hung his gunbelt on the bedpost, within easy reach. That done he begin to remove his clothes.

"Wait!" she said.

"What is it?"

"I like that you're being careful," she said, "but you're also going too fast."

"Isn't Gustav going to wonder where you are?" he asked. He hadn't necessarily believed the man when he said he was going to Riverton.

"No," she said, "he never does."

She came up to him and the heat from her body grew even more intense. Plus the aroma she gave off was heady. She got down on her knees, and undid his belt, and the buttons on his trousers, then eased them down until his hard cock jutted out.

"Yes!" she said, her eyes shining.

She dropped his pants and underwear to his ankles, took his penis in both of her hands and lovingly fondled it. She pressed it to her face, brushed her cheeks with it, then rubbed it over her massive breasts and nipples.

"Most of the men around here would be in me already, pounding," she said, missing the spongy head, "and finished in minutes."

"Well," he said, "this is going to take a lot longer than that, I guarantee . . . whoa--"

She took his cock into her mouth, cutting him off, bobbing her head back and forth, just letting him glide in and out over her lips, wetting it so that it gleamed.

Then she grabbed his hips, turned him and pushed him into a seated position on the edge of the bed. From there she yanked off his boots and tossed his clothes into a corner. He was completely naked, then, and she went back to his cock and this time her head didn't bob back-and-forth, but up-and-down on him.

"Jesus, you're good at that," he said, reaching down to run his hands over her smooth skin.

She looked up at him and smiled. "We can do anything you want. I'm not like many Western women. I have no limits."

"Well," he said, "we're going to find out, aren't we?"

She came up at him, then, pressing herself against him as she kissed, and still locked in the kiss worked them up on the bed.

All of her weight was on him and he didn't mind at all. It came with that hot, smooth skin. She was like acres of silk.

She kissed him hungrily, then worked her way down over his chest and abdomen with more kisses until she was once again between his legs. But once there she simply kissed his cock, and then mounted him and rubbed her wet pussy up and down the length of it before taking him inside in one quick movement.

"Oof," was the sound he made as she engulfed him, and if her skin was hot, her insides were scalding. He'd experienced the heat of many women, and he didn't know if it was because they were in Minnesota where it was colder, but this was more than intense.

She began to ride him, sitting up straight so he could see her breasts bouncing as she did. He reached for them, held them in his hands. But then he had to take hold of her hips, trying to match her rhythm.

She wanted to be in charge, obviously, and he was going to let her for a while, but it wouldn't last. He was just biding his time, enjoying the way her big breasts were flopping around right in front of his eyes. The more excited she got, the longer and harder her nipples seemed to get, and at one point he thought they might even be getting darker.

"Oh God, you feel so good inside me," she gasped, leaning forward to put her breasts in his face.

And now was the time.

Chapter Twenty-Eight

He knew it would be no easy task, but he managed to flip her onto her back, even though she was trying to resist.

"Put it back in, put it back in," she pleaded.

He gave her what she wanted, pressing his penis to her wet, gushing pussy lips and then ramming himself into her. She gasped, her eyes wide, and arched her back.

He drove it in and out of her then but remembered what she had told him about the men she'd been with doing that and finishing fast.

He slowed down, started fucking her in long, easy strokes. She raked his back with her nails as he leaned down to bite and suck on her nipples, which felt like big grapes in his mouth.

Finally, he withdrew his dick from her and scooted down so that he was between her thighs. He kissed their smooth, tender skin, then spread them even more and pressed his face to her golden patch.

"Hey," she said, "nobody around here does that—at least, not right."

"Well then you're in for a real treat," he said, "and so am I."

As his tongue probed through the hair, her body jerked, as if struck by lightning. He lapped at her, capturing all the nectar on the outside, and then went looking for more.

"Oh, Jesus," she said, lifting her butt off the bed.

He slid his hands beneath her butt cheeks and cupped them, bringing her up off the bed so he could get even closer. When he had his face buried in her he busied his tongue and she began to twitch and jerk and coo. Suddenly she was in a frenzy on the bed, whooping and hollering as if they weren't in a hotel with people in other rooms, but there was nothing he could do to quiet her except finish her . . .

***

"Oh Lord," she said later, when they were lying side-by-side. "I've been with a lot of men, but . . . not like that."

"You're quite a woman," he said.

"Except we're not done, right?" she asked, turning toward him. "I mean, you're not done."

"Oh no," he said, "I'm not done. Not by a long shot."

They rolled together and started kissing, and before long were at it again, straining against each other, looking for their own pleasures while also giving.

This time when she took him in her mouth she didn't stop sucking on him until he had exploded and she had milked him dry . . .

***

"Wow," he said. Once again, they were lying together catching their breath.

"You know, I think Gustav would be very happy about this."

"Really? I need to hear your reasoning."

"After this I don't want the men around here," she said. "This is it. You have ruined me for other men."

"That's a shame," he said. "It's going to make me feel guilty when I have to leave."

"When is that?" she asked. "When are you leaving?"

"I don't know," he said. "There are some things here I have to find out about."

He turned his head and looked at her. She was looking away, but her eyes were moving. He had the feeling she was trying to come to some sort of decision. Then she turned her head and looked back at him.

"So not soon, right?"

"No, not soon."

"And not tonight."

"Oh, no, not tonight."

She put her hand on his belly, moved it down and took hold of his cock. Instantly it started to swell again.

"Oh my," she said.

They rolled together and were going again . . .

***

Later she kept her word about having no limits.

She turned around on the bed, got on all fours and presented him with her majestic butt.

"Do what you want," she said. "The men around here don't know what to do with it."

111

"I think I can figure it out," he promised.

He got behind her, slid his long, hard dick up between her thighs and into her pussy from behind. She caught her breath and began to move with him as he pumped in and out of her. But he only did that until he was good and wet, then withdrew.

"Oh, God," she said.

He took hold of her ass cheeks and spread them so he could see her brown hole, then pressed the head of his cock—moist and slick with her juices—right up against it and pushed. It popped into her, and he slowly pushed the rest of his length in behind it, until he was completely engulfed.

He started to move, slowly at first, and then faster, until her flesh was jiggling. He could hear her breasts slapping against each other, and see the ripples going through her butt cheeks.

No limits, he thought, closing his eyes and looking for his own release . . .

Chapter Twenty-Nine

Hildegard Vanderhoff did not expect to be smitten with the Gunsmith.

She expected to use him like she used other men, and then walk away. Only lying beside him, trying to catch her breath after multiple sessions—four men could not have given her what he had given her over the past hours—she realized she was completely taken with him. How in the world, she wondered, could she get him to take her with him when he left? Not forever, just until they had worn each other out good and proper.

"What do you want to know?" she asked.

"What?"

"You said there were things you had to find out," she replied. "Are they about my husband?"

"Your husband," he said, "the town, the High Commissioner, and a man named DeVries who's actually named Collier."

She laughed shortly, but there was no humor in it.

"Is that all?"

"So far."

"What do you think you know so far?" she asked.

Clint looked at her, then sat up and swung his feet to the floor. If they were going to have a serious conversation, he needed to be dressed.

She watched as he put his clothes back on, then sat on the edge of the bed, still within reach of his gun.

"I think this is a town for outlaws," he said. "I think your husband and maybe some others wanted men to come here and start over, supposedly as Dutch shop owners or workers. The town is set up as Little Amsterdam so anyone riding in—like me—will realize it's a little different, but for obvious reasons."

"And that is true." With her back against the bedpost, her arms folded over her breasts, she asked, "Why does it matter to you?"

He couldn't answer that right away.

"Are you a lawman?"

"No."

"A reformed outlaw?"

"No."

"Then I don't understand your interest."

"To tell you the truth, neither do I," he said. "I suspected something was going on, something was off. If I find out I was right, then I could just ride on and be done with it."

"Exactly."

"So if you now confirm what I said, I should just saddle up and go."

"And take me with you."

"What?"

"I hate it here," she said. "You are right. It is not Dutch town, built to give people a happy and pleasant place to live. That is a lie that is drummed into everyone who comes here, so they'll remember."

"What about the foreman and hands on the ranch?" he asked.

"They work for my husband," she said. "They know about the town, but they live on the ranch, so they don't care. If they want to gamble they go to Riverton."

"You mentioned that you and your husband are from Philadelphia? Not overseas?"

"No, that is a lie, too," she said. "Gustav got in trouble in Philadelphia, decided to leave and start over someplace. He chose Minnesota and decided on this Little Amsterdam idea. We are Dutch, but we've never been to the Netherlands. My parents were born there. They're dead. I have no one but Gustav, which is why I do the things I do. But you . . . you're unlike any man I've ever been with."

"Hilda, don't say you're in love with me."

"No, no, of course not," she said. "But you've opened my eyes, shown that there are better men to be had. All I have to do is leave here and find them."

"So leave."

"I can't," she said. "Gustav has all the money. He would never let me go."

"Even though you sleep around?"

"It doesn't matter," she said. "He owns me, no matter what I do. That's the way he looks at it."

"Tell me about De Jong."

"That's his name, but he's wanted in a few of the Southwest states. He came up here, met my husband, and they got along."

"So he made him the High Commissioner."

"Yes."

"Have you been with De Jong?"

She hesitated, then said, "Yes, and he is in love with me."

"Why not have him take you away?"

"He wouldn't," she said. "He wants to stay here, but he wants to take over from Gustav."

"Ah," Clint said, "is he going to kill him?"

"He doesn't have the courage," she said. "He'll wait for Gustav to die or get killed. Maybe he even wants you to do it."

"You better get dressed," he told her.

She didn't argue. He thought things over while she put her dress back on.

"Okay," he said, "I guess I can go."

"And take me with you?"

"Yes," he said.

"Gustav will come after us."

"How far will he go?"

"To get me, his property back?" she asked. "To the ends of the earth."

He thought about that.

"I know," she said, "I'm talking you out of it."

"No, no," he said, "this will just take some planning. Give me a couple of days. Meanwhile, I'll continue trying to teach Gustav to shoot."

"Aren't you worried you'll teach him too well? And he'll be dangerous?" she asked.

"No," he said, "he's completely hopeless with a gun. No natural ability, at all. So there's no danger of his getting too good." He looked at her. "You better go home, Hilda."

She started for the door, then stopped.

"You won't leave without me, will you?"

"No," he said. "A promise is a promise."

She nodded, smiled and left.

Clint wondered what the hell he was doing, agreeing to help a wife run away from her husband? But this wasn't a normal husband-and-wife situation. And this certainly wasn't a normal town.

Chapter Thirty

Clint decided he needed a beer. And he needed to talk the situation through with somebody, so he could hear it out loud.

He got dressed, left the hotel and walked to the Bottom Saloon, it was getting dark. When he got there, he saw one of the batwing doors hanging by a single hinge. He put his hand on his gun and entered.

The place was a shambles. Tables and chairs had been overturned, bottles and the mirror behind the bar were broken. Then he saw several bodies on the floor. He drew his gun, took a good look around to be sure nobody was hiding, even checked the back room. Cautiously, he went back to check the bodies. They were the customers he usually saw in the saloon, and they were all dead.

He heard a whimper which seemed to come from behind the bar. He walked over to look behind it, and saw Miley sitting on the ground near Frank Kelton's dead body. Like the other men, he had been shot.

"Miley!" He holstered his gun and crouched down by her. "Are you hurt?"

"N-no, I don't think so."

"What happened?"

"I-I'm not even sure," she said, her face covered with the tracks of her dried tears. "I was upstairs where I have a room to change in, and I heard voices shouting. I opened the door to see if I could hear what was going on. Frank was telling someone to get out of his place.

"He said 'if you wanna know about the Gunsmith, ask him yourself.' And told him—or them—to get out again."

"I told you two not to get in trouble over me," he said.

"Frank is—was a stubborn man."

"Let me help you up," he said. "Are you sure you're all right?"

"Clint, I wasn't down here, I was upstairs when the shooting started."

"How many men were there?"

"It sounded like an army." she answered. "When the shooting stopped I came down and . . . and saw this. I ran to Frank, but he was dead."

"I can see where they might have gotten into it with Frank and shot him, but why these others? They were just in the wrong place at the wrong time."

"I was sitting by Frank's body when I heard you come in. I thought it might be them coming back, so I didn't move."

"Well, you're okay now," he said. "But you better come with me."

"Where? Why?"

"I can't let you go home," he said.

"But I didn't see anything."

"Nobody knows that," Clint said. "Whoever sent them over here is going to ask about you. When they say they didn't kill you, he's likely to tell them to come back and find you. We have to leave now!"

"Shouldn't we tell the sheriff?" she asked. "Or the, whataya callit, the High Commissioner?"

"Let me get you someplace safe," he said, "and then I'll go and talk to him—but I wouldn't be surprised if he knows about it already."

***

"You did what?" Commissioner De Jong exploded.

"I thought he was going for a shotgun under the bar," Seth Wilkins said. "Ain't that right, boys?"

The other four men nodded, and one said, "That's right, boss. That's the way it looked."

"Tell me exactly what you did."

"We made it look like somebody got drunk and shot up the place," Wilkins said. "We wrecked it."

"Why'd you do that?"

"It's the kind of thing that would happen in a place like that."

"Just how many men did you kill?" De Jong asked.

The other men looked away.

"Well, the bartender," Wilkins said, "and, uh, three or four others who were there. Ya know, customers."

"How many, altogether?"

"Well," Wilkins said, "the bartender . . . and . . . four all told."

"And the girl?"

"What girl?"

De Jong closed his eyes.

"There's a girl who works there."

"We didn't see no girl, did we boys?" Wilkins asked his cohorts.

They all shook their heads, and one said, "No girl, boss."

"But did she see you?" De Jong asked.

"Uh, well, I dunno . . . if she wasn't there—"

"Get your asses back there and find that girl," De Jong said. "And take care of her."

"Take care—"

"Make sure she can't point you out."

"You mean--"

"Kill her!"

"Right."

The 5 of them started to file out.

"And don't kill anybody else!" De Jong shouted after them.

Chapter Thirty-One

Clint had a totally different mindset now.

No longer was he wondering what the hell he was doing there, why he was trying to look beneath the surface of what Little Amsterdam seemed to be. No, now that he knew what it was, and Kelton and his customers had been killed, it was all different.

He was determined to close them down.

But he wasn't going to be able to do it on his own. He needed the law, and he wasn't going to get that from De Jong.

He took Miley to her room to collect some things, and then to his hotel. But he knew he wasn't going to be able to leave her alone, there. He was positive the desk clerk would report to De Jong as soon as he could.

"What do we do now?" Miley asked, when they were in his room. She sat on the bed with a single carpetbag containing all her belongings at her feet.

"We have to get out of here and find some real law."

"Riverton is the closest town," she said, "but it's still forty miles to the north."

"No," he said, "we can't go there."

"Why not?"

"Because that's where they'd expect us to go," he explained. "North to the nearest town. What's the next nearest one?"

"Well," she said, "there's Windham to the east about sixty miles, and then back over the border to the Dakota Territory, or even Iowa—"

"That won't do," Clint said. "If we tell the law there what's happening they'll say it's not their jurisdiction. We need to go someplace in Minnesota."

"Then I suggest Windham," she said. "From what I've heard from travelers, they have law, and a telegraph office."

"Windham," Clint repeated. "Sixty miles, huh? Do you have a horse?"

"No."

"Then we'll need to get you one," he said. "In fact, we'll need two more."

"Why?"

"There's somebody else who wants to get out of this town," he explained.

"Who's that?"

"Hildegard Vanderhoff."

Miley looked shocked.

"You're kidding."

"I'm not," he said. "She confirmed for me that this is an outlaw hideout, on the condition that I take her with me when I leave."

"But her husband founded the town."

"And if you want to live here and run a business, you have to pay him."

"You mean the fee Frank paid—"

"Went right into Gustav's pocket."

"Well, I'll be—so was it Gustav who had Frank killed?"

"I'm not sure," Clint said, "but I'm going to find out. First, I have to put you someplace where you'll be safe, and this hotel isn't it."

"Then where?"

"I've been giving it some thought," he said, "and you're probably not going to like it."

He told her.

And she didn't like it.

***

Clint had not made definite plans with Hilda on where to meet with her. Now he wished he had, for he had an audacious idea about where to hide Miley. But he was going to have to discuss it with Hilda, first.

Which meant getting her alone, again.

Chapter Thirty-Two

They had to spend the night in Clint's room. Once again he stuck the wooden chair underneath the doorknob.

The bed still smelled of his sex with Hilda, but Miley didn't seem to mind it. In fact, he had the feeling the aroma excited her. Sex in bed with the girl was even better than sex in the alley had been, and he was able to perform well enough despite the time spent with Hilda.

By morning Clint still hadn't figured out how to get a message to Hilda. But he knew he was going to spend some time again that day with Gustav, out at the ranch, giving him shooting lessons. Undoubtedly, he'd see Hilda there. He was going to have to try to get her alone for five minutes.

"And what do I do?" Miley asked.

"They're going to look for you at the saloon, and your room. It will take them a while to decide that you're with me. You can stay here with the door locked and I'll give you a gun—"

"I don't like that plan. What else you got?"

"Come with me to Gustav's ranch," Clint said. "I'll introduce you and tell him I promised to spend time with you."

"What'll he think?"

"You know what he'll think," Clint said, "unless word has gotten to him about what happened. And even if it has, you'll be there with me. I don't think he'll try anything."

"And if he does?"

"Then I'll handle it. The choice is yours, stay here or come along."

"I'll come along," she said.

"Okay then," Clint said, "do you have some riding clothes?"

"Yes, I packed 'em."

"Then put them on and we'll get you a horse."

"After breakfast?" she asked, hopefully.

He nodded. "After breakfast."

***

They rented her a horse at the livery and rode out to Gustav's Bar G ranch. His arrival with a girl in tow attracted the attention of hands by the corral. When he reached the house Gustav was waiting on the porch, and came down, with the Navy Colt tucked into his belt.

"You brought a guest," the man said, and his tone gave away nothing.

"Yes, I had promised Miley we'd spend some time together today. I hope you don't mind if she watches."

"Not at all," Gustav said, "Although it might be a little embarrassing for me. Hello, Miley."

"Hello, Mr. Vanderhoff."

"No, no, if you're a friend of Clint's then just call me Gustav."

"I'll just do that, Gustav."

"Have you picked out a place we can use?" Clint asked.

"Yes, behind the house," Gustav said, "and we have plenty of empty cans and bottles. You can leave your horses right here."

"All right."

Clint dismounted, helped Miley down from her rented mare and tied the horse off. He dropped Eclipse's reins to the ground.

"Lead the way," he told Gustav.

"Just give me a moment with my foreman," Gustav said, as Rance Edwards approached.

"Sure thing."

He walked over to confer with the foreman.

"I know him," Miley said, in a low tone. "He's been at the Bottom."

"Well, let's see if he knows you and says anything."

But when Gustav returned all he said was, "All right, let's go and shoot."

Clint had already decided he was going to show off in order to show Gustav what he'd be up against if push came to shove—or shoot.

When they got to the back of the house he saw that a sort of instant shooting range had been set up. Logs had been stacked up and on them were stacked a selection of empty cans and bottles.

"What do you think?" Gustav asked.

"Nicely done," Clint said.

"Is it far enough away?" Gustav asked.

"Let's see." Clint drew and fired six shots very quickly. Cans flew into the air, and six bottles shattered. He hurriedly reloaded and holstered the gun.

"Looks far enough," he said.

"My God!" Gustav said, in awe. "That was fast . . . and accurate."

"You said it," Miley added, also in awe.

"You'll find that speed isn't as important as accuracy," Clint told them. "Especially if you're facing another man with a gun, and not just shooting at empty cans and bottles for practice."

"Well," Gustav said, "I think I'll just stick with the targets."

Chapter Thirty-Three

Gustav was worse than ever.

The man had absolutely no aptitude for shooting. Clint even had him try a two handed shooting stance but he still didn't hit a thing.

"This is hopeless," Gustav finally said. "Even the great Gunsmith can't teach me to shoot."

"Well, you're a rancher," Clint said, "not a gunman. And you have men working for you who can shoot, right?"

"A few."

"We can try again another day."

"I've taken up too much of your time," Gustav said. "Two days worth of shooting and missing is enough."

"I suppose so."

"But come inside," Gustav said, "perhaps the young lady would like to have some lemonade?"

"That would be great," Miley said, because she knew that Clint wanted to get into the house.

They followed Gustav to a back door that led to the kitchen. The old lady he called Anneke turned from the stove and looked at them.

"You remember Clint," Gustav said.

She nodded and stared at him.

"And this is his friend, Miley," the rancher went on. "I'd like to give them both a glass of lemonade. Can we do that?"

She nodded again.

"Good, bring it into the living room, please."

The woman nodded a third time, and then they left the kitchen. When they got to the living room they found Hilda there, which pleased Clint.

"I heard shooting," Hilda said. "How did it go?"

"Badly," Gustav said. "I can't hit anything."

"That's too bad," she said, "and you have such a good teacher."

Then Hilda looked at Miley with curiosity.

"This is Clint's friend Miley. He brought her along to watch. We're going to have some lemonade.

"That sounds good," Hilda said. "I think I'll join you."

"Good," Clint said. "Maybe you and Miley can get to know one another."

Miley took the hint.

"This is a beautiful house," she said.

"Would you like to see the rest?" Hilda asked.

"I'd love it!"

"Anneke entered at that point with a pitcher of lemonade and 4 glasses.

"Let's take our lemonade with us, and I'll show it to you," Hilda said.

The two women grabbed a glass each and then left the room. Clint only hoped that Miley would have time to pitch their plan, and that she'd pitch it properly.

"Well, that leaves the two of us," Gustav said. "Tell me, if we give up on our shooting lessons, what will you do?"

"I'll probably move on," Clint said. "I think I've got an idea of what Little Amsterdam is all about."

"Do you?"

"Well, sure," Clint said. "Enough people have told me. It's a happy and healthy place to live, right?"

"That's exactly right. That was the plan."

"And it looks like it worked out perfectly for you," Clint said.

"How do you mean?"

"I mean," Clint said, "you've got exactly the kind of town you wanted . . . don't you?"

"I think I do," Gustav said, "but a drifter riding through might think otherwise."

"Well then," Clint said, "that drifter won't stay, will he?"

***

Either Gustav had no idea what had happened in town at the Bottom, or he was very casual about it. It seemed as if he was trying to give Clint a chance to ride off on his own. But Clint couldn't help but think Frank Kelton had been killed because of him. Maybe simply because he talked to him. Why, then, would they want to let Clint just leave town?

And he was in a perfect place for them to bushwhack, except he never would have come there if he thought the ranch hands were also gun hands. If Gustav was running an outlaw town, Clint had a feeling the ranch was separate from it. That being the case, the man wouldn't want to involve his hands in town business.

He did feel like he was fencing with words with the man, though. Maybe Gustav was doing to him the same thing he was doing to Gustav, just probing to see what he knew.

But by the time Hilda returned with Miley, no major information had been exchanged, and neither man had suffered a slip of the tongue.

"Have you seen the rest of this house?" Miley asked him. "It's so beautiful, and big."

"No," Clint said, "I'm afraid I'm not interested in how big somebody's house is. I think we better get going, Miley." He looked at Gustav. "She has to get to work."

"Oh?" Hilda said. "Where do you work?"

Miley looked at Clint.

"She works at a saloon called the Bottom." He looked at Gustav again. "Have you heard of it?"

Chapter Thirty-Four

Gustav was very good.

He didn't blink.

"That's Frank Kelton's place, isn't it?" he asked.

"That's right," Miley said.

"Tell Frank I said hello," he said to her.

"Frank never told me he knew you," she said.

"He had to talk to me when he got to town, before he was allowed to open his place."

"Oh," she said.

"I don't think I've seen him since he opened," Gustav went on, "but he'll remember me."

"I'm sure he will," Clint said. "Let's go, Miley."

Gustav and Hilda walked them to the front door, stepped out onto the porch with them. At the bottom of the stairs a few hands were inspecting Eclipse, but not getting too close to him.

Clint and Miley walked down, mounted up, waved at the Vanderhoffs, and rode off. They didn't speak until they were well out of earshot and sight of the house.

"What did Hilda have to say?" he asked.

"She believed me, said where to meet her later, and that she'd hide me."

"In the house?"

"Yes," Miley said, "but isn't that takin' a big chance?"

"It's the one place they won't look. Where did she say to meet her?"

"She says she sometimes rides the south range of the ranch, which almost takes her over the border. She suggests I meet her there in an hour. Then she says we can talk about it some more."

"Okay," Clint said. "We might as well ride down there now. If we're early we'll be able to see if she's being followed."

"Good idea," she said.

As they rode she spoke again.

"You made a big impression on her."

"Did I? What about you, did I make an impression on you?" he asked.

"A huge one."

"Good."

"You've been to bed with both of us."

"Well . . ."

"That's okay, you don't have to say anythin'," Miley said. "She's been to bed with most of the men in town—except, I think, Frank."

"I know that," he said. "I'm just helping her get away from a bad situation."

"A bad marriage?"

"And this town," Clint said. "I'm taking you both away from here."

"Well, the sooner the better."

"Where'd she say to meet, exactly?"

"She gave me directions," Miley said, jerking the reins on her horse. "I'll take the lead."

The meeting place Hilda had picked was a copse of black spruce that sported thin leaves with sharp needles.

"She said she spotted these while ridin' out this way," Miley said, as they reined in.

"Let's hope she comes," Clint said.

"You don't think she will?"

"Let's just say I'm not so trusting around here," Clint said.

"What about me?"

"I can't see any reason why you would lie," he said. "She might be a little different."

"Then why did you agree to help her?" Miley asked. "And decide to hide me with her?"

"I still can't think of a better idea," he admitted.

He dismounted and helped her down.

"Well," she said, looking around, "at least it's a pretty spot. You know, with no trouble at all we could be in Nebraska. Why don't we just go from here? I mean, since you're open to better ideas."

"I need to put this in the hands of somebody who'll have jurisdiction," he said. "That means staying in Minnesota. But . . ."

"But what?"

"But you and Hilda can ride to Nebraska," he said. "Or you could go yourself."

"No thanks," Miley said. "I'll stick with you until I'm sure nobody's gonna be chasin' me."

"Okay, then," Clint said, "grab a clump of ground and lean up against one of these trees, and we'll wait."

Chapter Thirty-Five

Hilda was true to her word and arrived within twenty minutes. She was dressed unlike Clint had ever seen her, in riding clothes.

"You know this is a crazy idea, don't you?" she asked Clint.

"I do know that," he said, "but can you think of another place they'd never look for her?"

"What happened?"

Clint told her about the massacre at the Bottom Saloon, and how they were probably looking for Miley in order to finish the job.

"Do you think Gustav sent them?"

"Either him, or De Jong."

"Probably De Jong," she said. "Gustav leaves those things to him."

"Same difference then," Clint said. "They're both behind it."

"But why do it in the first place?"

"Probably my fault," Clint said. "I'd been spending time there, and I think they wanted to know what I was talking about. Frank, the owner and bartender, wouldn't tell them a thing."

"I heard them yelling from upstairs," Miley said, "and then I heard the shooting. When I came down, Frank was dead and so were his three regular customers."

"Horrible," Hilda said.

"Hilda," Clint asked, "when did you first find out that Little Amsterdam was to be an outlaw hideout?"

"After we moved here, and the house had been built," she said. "There was nothing I could do then, so I just started . . . living my life, doing what I wanted to do."

"And now you're ready to leave?" Miley asked.

"Yes, as soon as Clint is ready."

"I need to make sure that we have some time when we leave," he said.

"Time for what?" Hilda asked.

"Time to get to Windham and turn this over to the law."

"And how do you propose to do that?" Hilda asked.

"I'm not sure," he said, "but I think I'm going to drop in on De Jong. I want to see if he glosses over what happened or admits it."

"And if he admits it?" Miley asked.

"I think I'll lock him in one of his own cells," he said. "Maybe it'll take a while for somebody to find him."

"But not all day," Miley said.

"You're right, not all day," he agreed. "Okay, change of plan."

"Why don't you just kill 'im?" Miley asked. "Isn't that what you do?"

"No," he said, "it's not what I do."

Miley backed off. "I'm sorry, I didn't mean—"

"I know what you meant," Clint said, cutting her off. "Hilda, you just have to hide Miley while I take care of this."

"And then what?"

"Why don't we meet here later," he said. "How long will it take you to pack?"

"That depends on what I pack—" Hilda started.

"Just what you can carry on a horse."

"Not long, then."

"Okay. Meet me here in in the morning. They'll never expect us to go south, and then we can double back and head for Windham."

"Why Windham?" Hilda asked. "Why not Riverton?"

"Because it's the closest town," Clint said. "That's where they'll expect us to go, so they'll probably try to block the way."

"I see."

He mounted up.

"I'll see you both here tomorrow morning, around eight," he said.

"And what will you do if something happens and we are not here?" Hilda asked.

"Don't worry about that. If that happens, I'll come looking for you," Clint said. "I'm not going to be leaving without the two of you."

The women stood together, not touching, and watched as Clint rode off, back toward Little Amsterdam.

Chapter Thirty-Six

It was probably a bad idea to go back to town to face High Commissioner De Jong, but Clint didn't want the man to think he'd gotten the best of him, once he left.

He rode into town and headed directly for the Commissioner's office.

***

That morning the men who killed Frank Kelton had come back to De Jong's office, with their heads hanging.

"Well?"

"We looked for her all night," Wilkins said. "We couldn't find her."

"You checked where she lives?"

"We don't know where she lives, boss," Wilkins said, "but we looked all over town."

"Somebody must know where she lives," De Jong said, tightly. "Find them, and then find her!" He slammed his fist down on his desk.

"Yessir."

When Clint reached the man's office De Jong was still waiting to hear from his men.

As he entered the office Clint thought De Jong was surprised to see him.

"Am I interrupting?" Clint asked.

"No, no," De Jong said, "I've got nothing goin' on right now. What brings you in?"

"I've heard some news that had me worried," Clint said.

"What's that?"

"I heard a rumor at breakfast that the Bottom Saloon was shot up last night, some people killed. Is that true?"

De Jong looked down for a moment, then when he looked up had a sad expression on his face.

"It was pretty bad," he admitted. "I went over there, but it was too late."

"How many dead?" Clint asked.

"Four, including the owner, Frank Kelton. Did you know him? You'd been over there a few times, hadn't you?"

"I had," Clint said. "We talked, but I didn't know him well. Too bad, though."

"Yes, it was."

"Not the type of thing that happens in this town, is it?" Clint asked.

"No, never," De Jong said, "but if it was going to happen, it would have been at that place. I told Gustav we made a mistake allowing him to open."

"Why's that?"

"He just wasn't our type," De Jong said, "not what we were looking for."

"If I remember right there was a girl working there," Clint said. "Was she killed?"

140

"No, she wasn't there," De Jong said. "That is, her body wasn't there. We're looking for her to see if she saw or heard anything. You wouldn't recall her name, would you?"

"Sorry," Clint said, "I know I saw her standing at the end of the bar, but I only talked with the bartender. Seemed like a nice enough guy."

"It was the kind of place you'd find across the dead line of some of those Western towns—you know, you were there. And I'm sure you were in Dodge City and Tombstone during their hey days."

"I was, and I know what you mean," Clint said. "Well, I also came to tell you I think I'm going to be on my way."

"Leaving town?"

Clint nodded. "Seems like just in time, too. If there are shooters in town, I'll be a target."

"I know what you mean. Where are you headed?"

"Probably back to Nebraska," Clint said. "Minnesota's a little too cold for me."

"Nebraska's not much different."

"Then I'll keep going south," Clint said. "I prefer the Southwest, anyway. Like you said, Dodge and Tombstone, places like that are more for me."

As Clint headed for the door De Jong said, "Say, what happened with Gustav's shooting lessons?"

"He's hopeless," Clint said, "more likely to shoot himself in the foot. He better sick to ranching."

"Did you tell him that?"

Clint forced a laugh and said, "He told me."

As Clint walked to the door, it was he this time, who turned for one more remark.

"I never saw that you had any deputies. That is, if you called them deputies."

"We have no need," De Jong said. "I can do the job just fine by myself."

"It's that you said you had somebody out looking for the girl."

"Just some men I use for special jobs."

"Like shooting up a saloon and killing the owner?"

De Jong didn't hesitate. His hand went for his gun, but he was no match for Clint, who cleanly outdrew him. It took all his will not to kill the man, as he rarely pulled his gun unless he was going to use it. But even if Little Amsterdam was an outlaw town, this fellow was still the law.

"Use two fingers and drop it."

De Jong did as he was told.

"Now into the cell block."

Clint walked De Jong into a cell and locked it, having snagged the key off the wall peg.

"What are you doing?" De Jong asked.

"Come on," Clint said, "you and I both know you sent those men to kill Kelton and shoot the place up."

"What?"

"Okay," Clint said, "maybe you didn't send them there to kill him, but you sent them. They were asking him about me and he wouldn't talk. Things got out of line, and your men lost their heads. The girl saw it all."

Suddenly, De Jong's face changed. He looked like a different man, not the mild mannered Commissioner Clint had been dealing with. He gripped the bars tightly.

"I told them to find that girl!"

"They'll never find her," Clint said. "And I'm leaving to bring the law back here, Commissioner."

"I am the law, Adams," De Jong said. "I'm not sure what you think you know."

"I know most of the people here are wanted somewhere," Clint said. "A Federal Marshal will find out where."

"I knew you were trouble the day you rode in," De Jong said.

"Is that so?"

"But Gustav," De Jong went on, "he has to play his games with the Gunsmith."

"Tell me," Clint said, "nobody can shoot as bad as he does, right?"

"Oh, no, he's that bad," De Jong said, "that's why I wear the badge and not him. I probably should have shot him in the back a long time ago and taken over."

"Don't worry about it," Clint said. "Pretty soon there won't be anything to take over."

"Before that happens I'll track you down."

"You'll have to get out of this cell first. In fact . . . step back."

De Jong did so.

Clint unlocked the cell door, went in, told De Jong to turn around, then tied and gagged the man. He stepped outside and locked the door again, then tossed the keys into the office, where he heard them hit the floor.

"I'm sure somebody will be along soon to let you out," Clint said.

Chapter Thirty-Seven

He had to meet Hilda and Miley in a little over an hour. He went to his hotel to collect his saddlebags and rifle, then hurried through the lobby.

"Sir?" the clerk called. "Are you checking out?"

Clint turned at the door and smiled.

"Now why would I check out?" he asked. "This is such a happy, pleasant place to live."

He went through the door, mounted up and rode out of happy and pleasant Little Amsterdam.

***

He expected them to be at the meeting place before him, so when they weren't he became concerned. What if they had gotten caught and he had to ride into the ranch to get them? Gustav would try to stop him, but would Edwards, the foreman. Or the hired hands?

He checked his guns to be sure they were all in firing order. He would give the Colt New Line to Miley, but he hoped Hilda would arrive with a gun.

He waited a half hour before getting too antsy to sit any longer. He paced and watched the rise they'd have to come over. Once or twice he thought he heard horses, but it turned out not to be the case. Finally, he decided he was going to have to ride to the Bar G and find them. As he was mounting up, he heard the definite sound of horses, and then two riders crested the rise.

It was Hilda and Miley.

***

"Have you seen my wife?" Gustav asked, Rance Edwards.

"She just rode out," the foreman said, "with that other girl."

"What girl?"

"The one Adams came here with."

"The saloon girl?" Gustav knew that de Jong had men out looking for her. He thought it best to keep his mouth shut, since Adams and the girl had headed back to town. Now what was she doing out here, riding with Hilda? And why was Hilda going out again? She had just returned a while ago from a ride.

"Saddle my horse and yours," Gustav said. "We're going out."

"Yessir!" Edwards said. "And, uh, there was something odd . . ."

***

"I was getting worried," Clint admitted, as the women arrived.

"She was packing too much stuff," Miley complained.

Sure enough, Hilda had two carpetbags hanging from her saddle, one on each side. If anyone had seen her riding out that way, they'd know something was amiss.

"Did anybody see you ride out?" he asked.

"No," Hilda said.

"We don't know," Miley said.

"If they saw you with those bags . . ." Clint said, shaking his head.

"There are things in here I earned!" she insisted.

"All right, never mind," Clint said, mounting up. "Let's just get moving."

"South?" Hilda asked, as Clint started riding.

"Just to create a false trail," he said, "then we'll double back and head north." He looked at Hilda. "Does Gustav have any men who can track?"

"I'm not sure," she said, "but Rance might be able to."

"That figures," Clint said. "I was kind of hoping Rance wasn't in on this."

"I don't know if Rance is part of what's going on in town," Hilda said. "I do know that the High Commissioner is."

"I've got him in a cell," Clint said. "We have a head start until he's found and released."

He didn't want to complain again that if someone had seen Hilda leaving with two carpetbags, De Jong might get out a lot sooner than he'd hoped.

***

By late in the day they were north of Little Amsterdam, heading for Windham. Clint hoped the false trail they had left would be enough to fool Gustav, De Jong and whoever was doing the tracking.

"Can we rest?" Hilda asked. "My bottom is sore."

"I thought you did a lot of riding," Clint said.

"In the afternoon," she clarified, "for pleasure. Not . . . this!"

Clint looked at Miley.

"How are you doing?"

"I'm fine," she said.

Neither of the women's horses were sweating, but that could have been because of the coolness of the weather.

"All right," he said. "Let's rest here a few minutes. I'm just going to ride back a ways and check our back trail."

He turned and rode back while the two women dismounted. Hilda stood there rubbing her butt with both hands.

"You can't be holdin' us up, Hilda," Miley said.

"Hilda?" the woman said, arching her eyebrows.

"You want me to call you Mrs. Vanderhoff?" Miley asked. "Out here? Besides, you just left your husband, so I don't know if you're gonna have that name much longer."

"You know," Hilda said, "I only agreed to help you because Clint asked me. Otherwise I would have nothing to do with a harlot like you."

"Harlot?" Miley laughed. "That's funny comin' from a woman who slept with every man in Little Amsterdam."

"You cannot believe everything you hear," Hilda said.

"Okay," Miley said, "so not *every* man."

"And you are pure?" Hilda asked.

"Only by comparison to you," Miley said.

They heard Clint returning.

"And which of us do you believe he prefers?" Hilda asked. "And don't tell me you have not slept with him."

"All I know is he's gettin' both of us to safety," Miley said. "I don't much care who he sleeps with." The last part was a lie, but she wasn't about to let Hilda Vanderhoff know she was getting to her.

When Clint reached them he said, "Our back trail is clear, for now. Hilda, walk around a bit and then we'll have to get going again."

"I'm ready now!" Miley announced.

"So am I," Hilda said.

"All right then, mount up."

Hilda looked as if she was going to wait until Clint helped her into the saddle, but when Miley scampered up into her saddle with no trouble, Hilda also mounted her own.

"Let's move!" he commanded.

Chapter Thirty-Eight

"This ain't right," Rance Edwards said.

"What isn't?" Gustav asked.

They had followed Hilda's tracks to the copse of trees where she and Miley met Clint, and then followed the tracks of three horses from that point. But then Edwards reined in.

"Why would they go south?" he asked.

"To get over the border."

"Yeah, but why?" Edwards said. "If you think the rider they met here is Adams, what's he tryin' to do?"

"Turn us in?"

"Then he needs to do that in Minnesota."

"You're right," Gustav said, after a moment.

"So this is a false trail," Edwards said. "They're goin' north."

"What about east or west?"

"I think they're going to Riverton," Edwards said. "It's the closest town with law enforcement, and a telegraph."

"Riverton it is, then," Gustav said. "We better head back to town and get De Jog and his men."

"Sir, if it's all right with you," Edwards said, "I'll stay out here and pick up their real trail. I'll probably meet up with you on the way to Riverton."

"All right, Rance," Gustav said. "I'll get De Jong and head that way. But if you catch up to Adams, don't try to take him alone."

"Don't worry about that," Rance Edwards said, "I'm in no hurry to meet my maker."

***

When Gustav entered the High Commissioner's office and saw it empty he wondered where the hell De Jong was. Then he heard something, some muffled sounds coming from the cell block. That was when he found De Jong.

He went to the wall peg where the keys usually were, and it was empty. He had to look around the office before he found the keys on the floor, where Clint had thrown them.

Unlocking the cell, he took the gag off De Jong's mouth first, then started to untie him.

"What happened?" he demanded.

"Adams," De Jong said, "He wanted a head start."

"Why didn't he just kill you?"

"Because I'm the law," De Jong said. "Even in this town he didn't want to kill a lawman. That saved me."

They left the cell block together and De Jong picked his gun up off the floor.

"Where'd he go?" Gustav asked. "Did he say?"

"No."

"We followed a false trail that he left, heading south," the rancher said. "Rance thinks he's heading for Riverton, though."

"Closest town," De Jong said, "and they've got a sheriff and a telegraph. Good guess."

"Where are your men?" Gustav asked.

"Still out looking for that saloon girl."

"She's with Adams," the rancher said.

"That figures," De Jong said. "All right, then, we can take them at the same time."

"And Hilda."

"What?"

"She is also with Adams, leaving me, or so she thinks."

"Are you sure?"

"She was seen riding out with two carpetbags on her saddle, with the saloon girl. They met another rider south of my place. Who do you think that might have been?"

"All right, then," De Jong said. "Let's get this over with. Once we have the three of them back we won't need to worry about our town—just what to do with them."

"Don't bring them back," Gustav said. "We kill them."

"All of them?" De Jong asked.

Gustav nodded.

"All of them."

Chapter Thirty-Nine

"Can we make it today?" Miley asked Clint.

He turned and looked behind them, where Hilda was trailing.

"Not if we have to keep stopping for her to rest," he pointed out.

"You're talking about me," Hilda called out. "I can tell. I am sorry I do not ride as well as you."

"I get the feeling she's only ever ridden until she met up with a man," Miley said.

"Now, now . . ." Clint said. Then he turned to Hilda. "If we have to stop for you again, Hilda, we won't make Windham. We'll have to camp for the night. That'll give Gustav and De Jong a chance to catch up."

"But you said you put De Jong in a cell."

"I'll wager he's been freed by now, and they're on our trail."

Clint reined in, and Miley did the same. They waited for Hilda to catch up.

"But you said you left a false trail," Hilda complained.

"It won't take long for a good tracker to discover that."

"If I had known it would be like this I wouldn't have come," she said.

Both girls were wearing riding clothes and jackets, but Hilda still looked cold and miserable. Clint's jacket was fighting a losing battle against the cold, as it got later in the day.

"We might have to stop and build a fire, just so we don't freeze to death," he said.

"Minnesota nights are cold," Miley agreed. "Even in the fall. But a fire will make us easy to find, won't it?"

"Hopefully," Clint said, "when they discovered the false trail they decided we were going to Riverton. They'll have to get there to discover they're wrong."

***

Rance Edwards knew his guess was wrong.

Adams and the women weren't going to Riverton. They were going to Windham. They'd still have the law and a telegraph there. Edwards also knew he was going to have to try to get there ahead of them, and then, hopefully, notify Gustav who, by then, would probably be in Riverton.

Adams would not be able to move fast. Edwards could make it to Windham before them because he knew the way, and how to go around them. He certainly didn't want to run into the Gunsmith alone.

Windham it was.

***

De Jong and Gustav rode out of Little Amsterdam with Wilkins and three more men.

"When we meet up with Rance we'll have seven," Gustav said. "That should be enough to handle even the Gunsmith." He had his Navy Colt stuck into his belt.

"I hope you're right," De Jong said.

***

Clint finally decided they had to camp. He'd just have to stay on watch all night.

"I'll take a turn," Miley told him, when they were seated around the fire.

They'd left in a hurry, but Clint always had at least coffee and beef jerky in his saddlebags.

"No," Clint said, "you and Hilda have to rest, I'll be fine. I've done this before."

"And what if you drift off to sleep?" Hilda asked.

"Eclipse won't ever let anyone sneak up on our camp."

"Eclipse?" Hilda said.

"His horse," Miley told her.

"Oh. We have to trust our lives to a horse?"

"Not just any horse," Clint said. "Don't worry. Just eat, and then turn in."

She stared at the piece of jerky he'd given her, and bit into it carefully. Both Clint and Miley were chewing hungrily.

After their meager meal, both women settled down to get some rest, although Hilda complained about sleeping on the ground. At this point Clint thought she might happily go back to her husband, given the chance.

Gustav, De Jong and his men pushed their horses hard and made it to Riverton by nightfall. They dismounted in front of the Four Leaf Saloon.

"You go and find the sheriff," Gustav said, "and tell him we're a posse hunting a man and two women. That's all he needs to know."

"Right."

"And don't bother with the High Commissioner title," Gustav said. "You'll just have to explain it."

"I got it, Gustav."

"What about us?" Wilkins asked.

"We're going into the bar for a beer," Gustav said. "One beer, got it?"

"We got it, boss," Wilkins said.

Chapter Forty

When Rance Edwards reached Windham he immediately went to the sheriff's office.

"A man and two women?" Sheriff Markus repeated. "No, nobody like that. You a lawman, son?"

"No, sir," Edwards said, "I'm the foreman of the Bar G over near Little Amsterdam."

"Amsterdam, huh?" Markus said. "I ain't never been there. Is that a big spread, the Bar G.?"

"Yes, sir. We're helpin' the law track these people down."

"What'd they do?"

"One of our saloons got shot up, the bartender and customers were killed."

"Jesus. By these women?"

"No, they're saloon girls, and we need to talk to them. But we think the man with them did it."

"I wish I could help, but there's nobody in town like that."

"Well, I tracked 'em and I think they're on their way here, and our sheriff is going to Riverton. I need to send a telegram there."

"The telegraph office opens at eight a.m.."

"I need to send it now," Edwards said.

"Son," Sheriff Markus said, "if our telegraph office don't open til eight, then neither does yours. You'll just have to wait."

Edwards did some quick thinking, decided the lawman was right.

"Yeah, okay," he said.

"You need some rest. You can pay for a hotel, but my cells are empty. You can have one of them, if you want."

"Thanks, Sheriff," Edwards said. "I appreciate that. I'll take care of my horse and be back."

"I'll get something from the café before it closes, bring it over here."

"Again, much obliged."

Rance Edwards left the lawman's office.

***

Gustav saw De Jong enter the saloon, look around, spot him and start over. The other men were further down the bar, drinking their one beer very slowly.

"What have you got for me?" Gustav asked.

"Nothing," De Jong said. "The sheriff said a man with two women hasn't ridden into town."

"So they didn't get here, yet."

"Maybe," De Jong said. He picked up the beer Gustav had bought for him and sipped it.

"What do you mean, maybe?"

"If they're even coming here."

"Where else would they go?"

"They could have gone south, maybe as far as Sioux Falls."

"No," Gustav said, "no one there would have jurisdiction. They have to stay in Minnesota."

"West would mean another border, so they either went east, or north."

"And north means here," Gustav said, "or Windham. There are no other towns with both law and a telegraph."

"And where's Rance?"

"If Rance followed Adams' trail it may have led him to Windham."

"Then he'll send a telegram," De Jong said. "We have to stay here til morning."

"Damn," Gustav said. "If Adams gets to talk to a lawman, we are in for trouble."

"Little Amsterdam is in for trouble," De Jong said. "You're just a rancher who lives in the area."

"And you?"

De Jong shrugged.

"I'm just doing the job I was hired to do."

"Well," Gustav said, "let's get this done so we don't have to deal with questions."

"I have a question."

"What is it?" Gustav asked, after a sip of beer.

"It's about Hilda."

Gustav stared at the man.

"You want her?" he asked.

"Well . . . if you're going to kill her . . ."

"You can have her," Gustav said. "If this ends up the way we want it, with Adams dead, then Hilda is yours to do with as you wish."

And in De Jong's mind, that only left one more thing for him to accomplish. After they killed Clint Adams, and he claimed his prize, he had to figure out when and where to kill Gustav Vanderhoff and take over Little Amsterdam.

"I'm going to get some hotel rooms," Gustav said. "One for me, one for you, and one for them to share. I feel I should pay for them, but not one each."

"That's fine," De Jong said. "We'll get an early start come morning."

"Yes," Gustav said, "but to where?"

Chapter Forty-One

In the morning Clint woke both women. Hilda had slept all night, while Miley had awoken, and offered to stand watch and let Clint sleep.

"I'm good," he told her. "Go back to sleep," which she did.

There was no coffee in the morning, just some water and beef jerky, which Hilda complained about.

"I'm hungry!"

"You can eat when we get to Windham. We need to get moving."

With Hilda still grumbling they mounted up and started out again.

***

That morning a knock came at Gustav's door. When he opened it a telegraph clerk was standing there.

"Uh, is your name Gustav . . . Gustav . . ." he squinted at the telegram. "Van—Vander—"

"Yes, that's me!" Gustav snapped.

"This came first thing this morning, marked urgent." The clerk handed it to him.

Gustav snatched it and closed the door in the man's face. After he read it he left his room to go to De Jong's door and pound on it.

"What?" De Jong said, opening it, fully dressed. "Oh, it's you."

"A telegram from Rance," Gustav said, holding it up. "Adams is not in Riverton."

"Then it's Windham," De Jong said. "It's got to be."

"Get the men. We're heading out. It's only twenty miles."

"The men are going to want to eat," De Jong warned.

"Tell them they can eat when we get to Windham," Gustav said. "I will pay."

"I'll get them," De Jong said, stepping into the hall with Gustav and closing his door.

"I'll go down and check us out. We'll meet in the lobby," Gustav said.

"Right."

***

After Rance Edwards sent his telegram to his boss in Riverton, he settled down in a chair in front of his hotel to wait. As soon as Clint Adams and the two women rode into town, he would duck out of sight.

This was going to end today.

***

"What are we going to do when we get there?" Hilda asked.

"Go right to the sheriff's office and tell him about Little Amsterdam."

"Will he believe you?"

"Well, I have you both to back my story," he said. "Miley can tell him about the shooting, and you have a lot to say about Gustav . . . don't you?"

"I guess . . ."

"What do you mean, you guess?"

Miley heard him raise his voice and looked over. They were riding abreast, with Clint in the middle.

"I wanted to get away," Hilda said, shaking her head, "but . . ."

"But what, Hilda?" Clint asked. "Come on, tell me what's going through your head."

"What's going on?" Miley asked.

Clint held his hand up to her, signaling for her to wait a minute.

"I—I just don't know if I can betray him," Hilda blurted out.

"Hilda," Miley said, leaning forward to look past Clint at Hilda, "you're a big part of this. You have to back Clint's story."

"But Gustav is my husband!" she wailed.

"Who you don't love," Miley said. "Right? I mean, you didn't care that he was your husband when you were sleepin' with all those other men."

Hilda didn't answer.

"But you're still afraid of him," Clint said.

Tears started to flow, and she rode on ahead.

"What's that about?" Miley asked. "And how can she be afraid of him. She cheated on him every chance she got, with every man—"

"He didn't care about that," Clint said.

"Then why is she afraid of him?"

"Because he doesn't like to lose things that he owns," Clint said.

"Like the town?"

"Like her."

"Well," Miley said, "if we get this done he's gonna lose both, and a lot more."

"She'll do it," he said. "She'll back our story with the law."

"I hope you're right."

Chapter Forty-Two

Rance Edwards wished that Gustav Vanderhoff's influence reached as far as the town of Windham. He was feeling very exposed, sitting there all alone. At least with a few men to back him he wouldn't be so vulnerable.

He wondered if he had time to walk around town, maybe hire a couple of guns for short term help. Just as he was about to stand up, though, he saw three riders coming down the street. He recognized Hilda Vanderhoff riding alongside Clint Adams. They had another woman who he knew would be the saloon girl.

He got up quickly and stepped into the hotel lobby. From there he continued to watch them ride down the street. He knew their destination was probably the sheriff's office. He knew once Adams talked to the sheriff, the lawman was going to have to be killed.

This had all been explained to him by Gustav back when he first hired him. Edwards knew what the town of Little Amsterdam was, but his job was as foreman of the ranch. He wasn't supposed to have to deal with anything that happened off the ranch, and he never had, up to this moment. But Gustav had put him in the field for a reason. He just hoped he was up to the job.

Clint's eyes raked both sides of the street. He didn't have any way of knowing if Gustav Vanderhoff had sent any men there, or if his influence reached here. He'd know more after he spoke with the sheriff.

They reined in their horses in front of the sheriff's office.

"Dismount," Clint said. "We're all going in."

He stepped down, as did Miley. Hilda remained in her saddle, staring at the front door.

"It's now or never, Hilda," Clint said. "This is your chance to get out from under Gustav's influence."

She stared at him, did some quick thinking, and then dismounted.

When they entered the sheriff's office the man behind the desk looked up at them in surprise. A man and two attractive women, looking like they'd ridden all night.

"Well," he said, "this should be interesting."

"You don't know the half of it," Clint said, and introduced himself . . .

***

"That's quite a story," Sheriff Jeff Markus said.

"It's true."

"And I suppose these pretty young ladies will back you up?" Markus asked.

"You'll have to ask them," Clint said, "but right now we better get ready. I'm sure they're on their way here to kill us, and maybe you, if you get in their way. You got a deputy?"

"Talk about gettin' killed, that's what happened to him last week," the sheriff said. "I ain't replaced him, yet,"

"Got anybody you can deputize?"

"Not right away," Markus said. "And I assume I'd have to do that now?"

"I'd advise it."

"Then I guess it's just gonna have to be me."

"Why don't you deputize Clint?" Miley asked.

The sheriff, a man in his 50's with a full grey beard looked at her and said, "I'd have to completely believe his story to do that, Ma'am."

"And you don't?"

"Why should I?" he asked. "I've heard of the Bar G, and Little Amsterdam. Haven't heard anything bad about either one."

"Until now," Hilda said. "My husband is a bad man, Sheriff."

"Yes, Ma'am," Markus said, "so you've been tellin' me."

"Sheriff—" Clint started.

"Why don't you get these ladies somethin' to eat, Adams?" Markus said. "The Buggy Seat Café is right down the street. You could all use some breakfast. I may not have a deputy, but I've got a judge in town, and a mayor. I'm gonna have to talk to them, and then they're probably gonna wanna talk to you before we do something like telegraphing for a Federal Marshal."

"A Federal Marshal will have to go into Little Amsterdam to clean it up," Clint said. "And it'll take time to get him here. Time which I don't think you have."

"Well," Markus said, "maybe I've got time to do what I need to do to keep my job."

"Sheriff—"

"The Buggy Seat," Markus said, cutting him off, "stupid name, but good food."

"Uh-huh," Clint said. "Is that all I'm going to get out of you?"

"For now."

Clint put one hand on each shoulder of the women who were seated in front him, facing the sheriff.

"Come on, ladies," he said, "we might as well go and get something to eat."

Chapter Forty-Three

"What do we do now?" Miley asked, while they were eating.

Some of the tables in the Buggy Seat Café actually had buggy seats as chairs, hence the name.

"Well, if the sheriff isn't willing to send a telegram to get a Federal Marshal here, I can do it myself."

"You know how to do that?" Hilda asked.

"I have some contacts, yes," Clint said. "It just won't be an official request."

"Can we do that after we eat?" Miley asked.

"Telegraph office should be open," Clint said, "so yeah, we'll try that."

After a while Hilda said, "There is something else you should know."

"About what?" Clint asked.

"Abraham De Jong."

"And what's that?"

"My husband has two things he wants."

"And they are?"

"Little Amsterdam," she said, "and me."

"Why are you tellin' us that?" Miley asked.

"I just thought perhaps it would be useful when dealing with them," she said. "I doubt that Gustav will come after us without Abraham."

"Is Abraham one of your many conquests?" Miley asked.

"That doesn't matter," Clint said. "The information might come in handy, Hilda."

Hilda nodded and looked away from Miley, who was glaring at her.

***

After they ate, Clint walked the two women to the telegraph office with him.

"Who are you sending a telegram to?"

"I have a friend who's a U.S. Marshal," Clint said. "His name is Custis Long and he works out of Denver. I'll see if there's anything he can do."

"How long will it take to get someone here?" Hilda asked.

"It'll take a while," Clint said.

"So what do we do until then?" she demanded. "Keep running?"

"You could always go back," Miley offered her.

She gave the younger girl a hard look.

"I am not looking to go back, but I am not looking to get killed, either."

"I'll send the telegram," Clint said, "and then find someplace safe to stash the two of you."

"And then what?" Miley asked.

"And then if Gustav and De Jong show up here, I'll handle it."

"They'll have men with them," Hilda warned.

"How many?" Miley asked her.

"Abraham has at least four or five that he uses," Hilda said.

170

"The same men who killed Frank, I'll bet," Miley said. She looked at Clint. "You can't face them alone."

"We'll see about that when they arrive," Clint said. "First let's get this telegram sent."

They all stepped into the telegraph office.

***

Rance Edwards watched as Clint and the women left the sheriff's office and walked to the telegraph office. That could only mean trouble. He had to find out who the Gunsmith was sending a telegram to, so he could tell Gustav when the rancher arrived with De Jong and his men.

He took up a position across from the telegraph office and waited.

***

Clint sent the telegram to the Denver, Colorado office of the U.S. Marshals, addressed specifically to Marshal Custis Long, who was known to many people as Longarm. It might be read first by Long's boss, Marshal Billy Vail, but it would get to him, eventually.

"What's the closest hotel to here?" he asked the clerk.

"That'll be Bensonhouse," the clerk said. "Right up the street."

"Will they have rooms?"

"They always have rooms."

"Then that's where you should bring my reply." Before the man could object, Clint handed him some extra money. "Same amount when you deliver."

"I'll run it right over myself, sir," the clerk assured him.

Clint and the women left the telegraph office and walked to the Bensonhouse Hotel, where Clint got them 3 rooms. He walked them each to their doors, which were down the hall from each other, and his.

"If I was you," he said to both of them, "I'd stay in my room until I come for you."

"And if you don't come?" Hilda asked.

"I'll be here," he assured her.

She entered the room and closed the door.

At Miley's room she said, "I agree with Hilda, Clint. What if you don't come back for us?"

"I don't know what Hilda will do," he said, "but you've been on your own before. But just in case, take this." He handed her the little Colt New Line. "If anybody but me comes through this door, shoot them."

"All right."

Impulsively, she hugged him.

"Please be careful."

Chapter Forty-Four

Race Edwards went to the telegraph office, and for more money than Clint had given the clerk, the man told Edwards who Clint's telegram had gone to.

"Is there any way you can get it back?" Edwards asked.

"There's no way," the man said. "Once it's been sent, it's sent."

"Okay, thanks."

After that Edwards went right to the sheriff's office.

"What story did he tell you?" he asked.

"It was pretty wild," Markus said, "but he did have two people supporting it."

"I told you when I got here, they're all on the run."

"So you did," Markus said, "but they were pretty convincin'. I mean, come on, you didn't tell me he was the Gunsmith."

"A gunman with his reputation?" Edwards said. "You're gonna believe him over Gustav Vanderhoff? A respected rancher?"

"When Mr. Vanderhoff gets here," Markus said, "I guess we'll see."

Edwards left the sheriff's office, unsatisfied. He started to cross the street, came up short when he saw Clint Adams coming right at him.

"Let's talk," Clint said.

After Clint left the girls in the hotel he went back down to the street, looked both way. He had spotted Rance Edwards earlier, watching them from a doorway, but he hadn't told them. He wanted to talk to the ranch foreman alone.

He was still standing in front of the hotel when he saw Edwards come out of the telegraph office. It wasn't hard to guess why he was there. As he watched, the man walked to the sheriff's office.

Clint quickly made a stop at the telegraph office, then crossed the street again to wait across from the lawman's office. When he saw Edwards come out, he immediately started across.

As he approached Edwards, the man looked up and saw him, going wide-eyed.

"Let's talk."

***

They walked down the street, past the telegraph office, to a saloon called The Corral. It was small, and just starting to get busy, offering drinks, girls and gambling.

They walked to the bar and Clint ordered two beers from the attentive young bartender.

"There you go, gents," the young man said. "Just let me know if you want anythin' else."

"Thanks," Clint said.

Edwards grabbed his drink and took a large gulp. He had almost expected the Gunsmith to just shoot him in the street, and he still wasn't sure he wouldn't.

"You made a good guess, Rance," Clint said, "or did you track us here?"

"I tracked you," Edwards said, "after I realized you left a false trail."

"So I guess you let Gustav and De Jong know we're here?"

"I sent a telegram to Riverton early this mornin'."

"So they'll be here any time."

"Yeah."

"With how many men?"

"I dunno," Edwards said. "Gustav, De Jong and some men."

"And you."

Edwards drank more beer.

"Out on the street," Clint went on. "All of us."

"I'm no gunman," Edwards said. "I tracked you. That's it."

"You think so?"

"Are you gonna kill me?"

"I'm going to kill any man who stands out in the street against me," Clint said.

"Well, that won't be me," the foreman said.

"You don't think Gustav is going to make you stand out there with him?"

"He knows I'm no gunman," Edwards said, "but I'll tell you one thing."

"What's that?"

"He is."

Clint smiled.

"You know, I thought nobody could be that useless with a gun," he said. "And the Navy Colt?"

"Oh, that's his gun," Edwards said. "He loves to use it."

"Well," Clint said, "it would blow a cannonball size hole in a man. And De Jong?"

"No gunman," Edwards said, "but better than me."

"And the other men," Clint said, "will they be the ones who killed Frank Kelton and the others?"

"They will be."

"That's good," Clint said, "because I owe them."

Chapter Forty-Five

Clint and Rance Edwards were sitting in front of the Corral Saloon when Gustav Vanderhoff, High Commissioner Abraham De Jong and four other men rode into town.

De Jong spotted them right away.

"Gustav," he said.

"I see them."

"What's Rance doing with him?"

"We will find out," Gustav said. "Just follow my lead, Abraham. Make sure your men do not fire unless I do."

"All right."

They started riding toward the saloon.

***

"There they are," Edwards said to Clint. "Can I go now?"

"No," Clint said, stay right where you are."

Edwards was wearing a gun, but it was crystal clear that he didn't want to use it.

Clint watched Gustav closely as the six men rode toward them. When they stopped them he just remained where he was, stayed relaxed.

"Hello, Gustav," Clint said, noticing the Navy Colt in the man's belt.

"Clint. Led us a merry chase."

"Not so much," Clint said. "I was hoping it would take longer."

"Where's the girl?" Gustav asked.

"Where's Hilda?" De Jong asked.

"Well, look there," Clint said, "it's the High Commissioner who's worried about your wife."

"She made her choice," Gustav said. "Why are you here with him, Rance? Did you make your choice?"

"Hell, no," Edwards said. "He's makin' me sit here. I told him I ain't no gunman, and you weren't gonna make me stand in the street with you."

"If you don't stand with me, Rance," Gustav said, "who are you going to stand with?"

"Nobody!" Edwards blurted out. "I did my job for you, Gustav. That ain't fair."

"So you think he's going to let you stand up and walk away because you don't want to be involved?"

"I don't know—"

"He can stand up and go whichever way he wants," Clint said. "His choice."

Edwards looked at Gustav.

"All right," the rancher said, "go or stay."

Carefully, Edwards stood, but didn't leave.

"Will I still have my job?" he asked Gustav.

"Why are you asking him?" Clint said. "He won't be around, and you will."

Edwards looked surprised at Clint's word.

"Go on, Rance," Gustav said. "Get out of here. We don't need you. In fact, get on your horse and head back to the ranch. I'll see you there."

Edwards, not wanting to be shot in the back, backed away and didn't turn until he was well away.

"Now, you, Adams," Gustav said. "In the street."

"Against all of you?" Clint asked. "Or just you and your pet lawman?"

"I'm nobody's pet," De Jong said.

"Oh, that's right," Clint said, "you've got your eyes on a couple of prizes, don't you, De Jong? You want Gustav's wife, and his town."

"What's he talking about?" Gustav asked.

"De Jong wants Hilda," Clint said.

"I know that," Gustav said to Clint, "and he can have her." He turned to De Jong. "What is this about wanting Little Amsterdam?"

"He's just taking, Gustav," De Jong said. "Don't listen to him."

Clint saw that the other four men were watching De Jong for his move, not Gustav. The rancher might not have realized he wasn't in charge.

"I see you've got your Navy Colt, Gustav," Clint said. "You going to stop playing useless with it?"

Gustav laughed.

"I thought that was pretty funny," he said, "but I'm probably still not a match for you, Adams. But together, we are a match."

The other four men were still looking at De Jong.

Gustav also looked at him. "Abraham, we'll talk about what you want after we finish what we came here to do."

"No, no, no," a woman's voice rang out.

All the men looked in the direction of the voice and saw both Hilda and Miley approaching the scene. It was Hilda who was shouting.

"Gustav, you must know what I know, that Abraham plans on taking Little Amsterdam from you, even if it means shooting you in the back."

Gustav stared at Hilda, then turned his attention to De Jong. The High Commissioner wasted no time. He drew his gun.

Chapter Forty-Six

Gustav Vanderhoff beat Abraham De Jong to the draw, even though his Navy Colt was in his belt, while De Jong's gun was in a holster. The High Commissioner was flung from his saddle, landing on the street with a thud.

The other four men, who had been watching him, also drew on Gustav. For a split second Clint thought about just watching the action play out, but then his instincts took over. Hoping that the two women would be smart enough to duck, he pulled his gun.

He fired twice, snatching two men from their saddles and depositing them on the street with their boss, De Jong.

Gustav had to cock and fire his single-action weapon, but he still managed to shoot the other two men off their horses. With the rest of the men taken care of Clint and Gustav turned their attention to each other, each holding their gun ready.

"Now what?" Clint asked. "You're all alone."

"I guess I was alone when I got here," Gustav said. He looked over at Hilda, as she and Miley got back to their feet. They'd taken cover behind a horse trough. "Thank you, my dear. I think you kept me from getting killed."

"Don't mention it," she said.

He looked at Clint.

"Who have you talked to?"

"The sheriff," Clint said, "who should be here shortly. I also sent a telegram to a U.S. Marshal I know."

"What did you tell him?"

"Nothing . . . yet."

"What are you going to tell him?"

"All about Little Amsterdam."

"I can't let you do that," Gustav said.

"If you try to stop me, it won't matter," Clint said. "You can't beat me, even though you're pretty good."

Gustav looked at the Navy Colt in his hand, then lowered it.

"I know that."

"Here comes the sheriff," Clint said. "Stick that in your belt." He holstered his Colt without reloading it, which was rare, but he'd take care of it later.

"What the hell's goin' on?" Sheriff Markus demanded. He looked at the two men, and the two women. Then at the dead men in the street.

"Just a little misunderstanding, Sheriff," Clint said.

"I think we're gonna have to discuss this misunderstandin' in my office." He looked at the crowd that had gathered. "Some of you men take these bodies over to the undertaker."

"Right, Sheriff."

"You four," he said to Clint, Gustav, Hilda and Miley, "come with me. Do I need to disarm you?"

"No," Clint said, "we'll come quietly."

"Indeed," Gustav said. "The gunplay is finished, Sheriff."

"Good to know. Let's go."

"I'm afraid I don't know what Mr. Adams, is talking about, Sheriff," Gustav said. "I'm a rancher, and I live near Little Amsterdam. That's all I know."

"Adams says it's an outlaw den," Markus pointed out.

"I don't know anything about that, I'm afraid."

"Uh-huh."

"He's lying," Hilda said. "He owns the town."

"Uh-huh. And you're his wife?"

"That's right."

He looked at Miley.

"And you?"

"I'm just a saloon girl."

"She was in the wrong place at the wrong time," Clint said. "That saloon where everybody was killed."

"By those men in the street?"

"I'd say yes, but I don't know for sure," Clint said.

"And the other man? He was the law in Little Amsterdam?" Markus asked.

"Yeah," Clint said, "but they called him the High Commissioner, and he's got no badge."

"I noticed that when he was lyin' out there," Markus said. "Guess I ain't gotta figure him for a lawman. That way you didn't kill one."

"I didn't," Clint said. "He did."

"That right?" Markus asked Gustav.

"Yes," the rancher said. "He left me no choice."

"He's right," Clint said, "De Jong—that's his name—drew first. And the others followed."

"And you two got them."

183

"We did," Clint said.

Markus looked at the two women.

"That's the way it happened," Miley said, and Hilda nodded.

Markus sat back in his chair.

"So what am I supposed to do?" he asked.

"Like I said before," Clint said, "call for a U.S. Marshal to look into the town of Little Amsterdam."

"I suppose I could do that," Markus said. "What do you think, Mr. Venderhoff?"

"I rather think that's not necessary," Gustav said, "but the final decision is up to you." Gustav stood up. Clint and the women remained seated. "May I go now?"

"Do you have business here in town?" Markus asked.

"I thought I did," he said, "but apparently, I was wrong."

"Okay," he said, "you and your wife can go home."

"I am heading home," Gustav said, "whether or not she comes is up to her. Good day, Sheriff."

"Yeah," Markus said, "good-day."

"Adams," Gustav said.

"Gustav."

The rancher walked to the door, put his hand on the doorknob, and turned back.

"Coming, dear?" he asked Hilda.

She looked at Clint and Miley and said, "I have to."

"It's up to you," Clint said.

"I'm coming," she said, and hurried after her husband as he went out the door.

"What's gonna happen to her now?" Miley wondered.

"I don't know," Clint said. "Sheriff, I sent a telegram to a U.S. Marshal in Denver. I don't know how that's going to pan out."

"Denver?"

"That's right."

"And he's a U.S. Marshal?"

"Yes."

"Well then, I guess I better send a telegram of my own."

Clint and Miley stood up.

"If that town's as dirty as you say," Markus said, "what do you think this Gustav will do?"

"I think he'll look out for himself," Clint said. "By the time the Marshals get there, he'll be gone, but I think the rest of them will still be there. The Marshals will end up closing out a lot of wanted posters once they're done. And you'll get some credit."

"What about you?"

"Me?" Clint said. "You don't even have to mention me. Take the credit yourself."

"Well," Markus said, "that's right nice of you."

"We'll be leaving town in the morning, Sheriff," Clint said. "Early. So this is good-bye."

The two men shook hands, and Clint and Miley left the office.

***

At their hotel the desk clerk handed Clint a telegram that had just arrived.

"Is that from your Marshal friend?" she asked, as Clint read it.

"Yes," Clint said, folding it back up. "He's going to take the proper steps to look into Little Amsterdam."

"So it's over?" Miley asked.

"Pretty much."

"What about Gustav and Hilda? Where will they go?"

"Someplace else," Clint said, "where they can be somebody else."

"Do you think they'll change?"

"I doubt it."

"And where will you go?" she asked.

"Out of Minnesota," he said, "that's for sure."

"I don't know where I'll go," she said, "but you were right about one thing."

"What's that?"

"I have been on my own before."

"You'll be fine."

They started up the stairs to the second floor. When they reached it Miley said, "Can we use one room, tonight?"

"I don't see why not," Clint said.

Coming Soon!

THE GUNSMITH
434
The Butcher of the Bayou

Visit us at www.speakingvolumes.us

On Sale Now!

THE GUNSMITH
432
The Bank Job

Visit us at www.speakingvolumes.us

On Sale Now!

THE GUNSMITH
431
The Science of Death

Visit us at www.speakingvolumes.us

On Sale Now!

THE GUNSMITH
430
Show Girl

Visit us at www.speakingvolumes.us

Coming Spring 2018

Lady Gunsmith 5
The Portrait of Gavin Doyle

For more information
visit: www.speakingvolumes.us

On Sale Now!

ANGEL EYES *series*
by
Award-Winning Author
Robert J. Randisi (J.R. Roberts)

Visit us at